"I'm not sure [...] *it,"* she said *suddenly, softly.*

"Manage what?"

"Staying out of trouble."

She turned around, ducked in her car. He stood there even after she'd backed out of the parking lot and zoomed down the street.

He was about eighty-eight percent sure that she'd just given him a dare. She hadn't *said,* "I want trouble." But her tone had a whispery dare in it. Her eyes had a fever-bright dare for damn sure. Her body, her smiles… Oh, yeah. She was all about danger and dares.

It wasn't a good idea to dare a guy at the end of his hormonal tether. He'd been good as gold, for Pete's sake. But like his four-year-old said—his *male* four-year-old—nobody could be good *all* the time.

Dear Reader,

I've set stories in the mountains, near the ocean, in small towns and downtowns, but for this book I wanted a different location. I needed a setting where two strong characters were tested to their limits...where only the strong survive...where the culture was exotic for both the hero and heroine. Y'all can guess what I'm talking about.

The Suburbs.

I had so much fun writing these characters! In one corner, we have Alpha-male Mike and his four-year-old alpha-male son, Teddy. In the other corner, we have two female redheads, both girlie-girl to the nth degree. For a while, I wasn't sure if they could make it...but as I've discovered in other stories...love really does find a way.

Hope you enjoy!

Jennifer Greene

Don't hesitate to write me, either through my website (www.jennifergreene.com) or through my Jennifer Greene author page on Facebook.

YOURS, MINE
& OURS

JENNIFER GREENE

Harlequin®

SPECIAL EDITION

Recycling programs
for this product may
not exist in your area.

ISBN-13: 978-0-373-65590-8

YOURS, MINE & OURS

Copyright © 2011 by Alison Hart

JENNIFER GREENE

lives near Lake Michigan with her husband and an assorted menagerie of pets. Michigan State University has honored her as an outstanding woman graduate for her work with women on campus. Jennifer has written more than seventy love stories, for which she has won numerous awards, including four RITA® Awards from the Romance Writers of America and their Hall of Fame and Lifetime Achievement Awards.

You're welcome to contact Jennifer through her website at www.jennifergreene.com.

For Lilly: Get ready, you sweetheart.
A life of wonders is just waiting for you.

Chapter One

Mike Conroy pulled down the tailgate of his white pickup. Brilliant May sunshine gleamed on the revolting heap of supplies in the back. He started unloading—first, the gray plastic bins. Then came the burlap, the shredded newspaper and the bags of soil.

Last, of course, came the worms.

He wasted a few seconds, rolling his stiff shoulders, mourning how his life had come to this. Even when he was a teenager, he'd had precise, clear dreams of what he wanted from life. He'd always wanted to be a successful lawyer—and he'd done that. He'd always wanted to live in a big city—and he'd done that. He'd always dreamed of living with a sexy, beautiful woman—and God knew, he'd done that, too.

He'd not only done all those things; he'd thrown that entire life away. But even at his lowest, he'd never anticipated wanting to start a worm farm. Ever. Even remotely.

"Hey, Dad. Isn't this *great?* Isn't this the best thing ever? Where are the worms? Can I see the worms?"

"Not yet, Teddy. We need to get them out of the sun, into the basement. You can help me set everything up."

"How soon do you think we'll have worm poop, Dad? You think *soon?*"

Mike knew well that when his four-year-old said *soon,* he was hoping the event would happen within the next three seconds. "The plan is to get all the supplies into the basement. Then to come upstairs, wash our hands, chill out with a glass of orange juice. And after that, the two of us can get our hands down and dirty creating our worm farm."

"Hey, Dad." Teddy, whose thatch of brown hair never looked brushed, who could put a hole in a new pair of jeans faster than lightning, who had a Tough Guy T-shirt with four separate food stains on it, looked up at him with adoration. "Worms are my favorite thing in the whole world. This is the best thing that happened to me in my whole life. I'm not kidding. I mean it. I'm not telling a story this time. It's *true,* Dad."

"I believe you, sport. In fact, that's exactly why we're doing this."

"And we're gonna make a pond. And have frogs and stuff."

"You bet."

"Mom would never let me do this."

Mike yanked the T-shirt over his head, tossed it on the truck seat.

Chicago springs were usually perfect, but this May had been a furnace. All afternoon, it'd been hot enough to choke. Sweat prickled the back of his neck. And no, he didn't respond to Teddy's comment about his mother. He was getting good—not perfect, but good—at refraining from criticizing Nancy in front of their son. He'd sworn never to make Teddy prey to those kinds of divorce battles.

"Hey, Dad—"

Thankfully he was saved another set of questions by the arrival of a white SUV zipping into the drive next to theirs.

He looked up. Teddy looked up. Even Slugger— the bassett hound snoozing upside down on the front porch—was curious enough to open one droopy eye.

He and Teddy had moved from downtown Chicago just two weeks before. Living anywhere near suburbia was another thing Mike had never planned to do, but that was another life-compromise emanating from the divorce. At least this neighborhood didn't look like Clone City. Silver Hills was a new suburb on the far west side, with all kinds of architecture and at least a half acre between most homes. His place was a modified A-frame, primarily redwood and glass, and richened up by a two-story stone chimney. The best part was being at the end of a cul-de-sac, with a serious deck and woodsy ravine in the back.

The closest house to the east had a Sold sign in the yard when they first moved in, but Mike hadn't seen any sign of life there until a few days before, when a moving van had pulled up and unloaded. Still, there'd been no sign of the owners until now.

The neighbor's house was fancier, built of field-stone, with two dormer windows upstairs and huge casement windows framing the center door. To Mike, it was a little pretentious, had kind of a fake country-estate look—not that it made any difference to him.

He missed a glimpse of the driver, because his attention was drawn by a child skipping around the back of the car. It was a girl. An ultra girlie-girl, about the same age as his Teddy. She was dressed to the gills in pink—a pink top with sequins and shiny beads and more shiny stuff attached somehow to her wildly curly red hair. The white pants had pink edges, and she had shoes that lit up with pink lights when she skipped around.

Teddy looked thunderstruck—but not necessarily

by the girl. The problem was that Slugger—who never moved fast unless a steak bone was in sight—spotted the girl and started baying nonstop. The little girl happened to have a dog next to her. At least, Mike was pretty sure it was a dog. It was white, possibly a cross between a miniature poodle and schnauzer, and just like the girl, it was gussied up beyond belief with a pink rhinestone collar and other jewelry items he'd never imagined on a canine before.

Slugger flew off the porch step and trundled over to greet the poodle with a cascade of more baying and howling. The poodle promptly squatted down and peed. Then Slugger peed. Then the dogs started chasing each other. All that might have gone fine, except that Teddy—his ever-friendly son—galloped over to the girl and began telling her all about their brand-new worm farm.

Teddy only had to say the four-letter *worm* word once for the girl to launch into a long, versatile scream that could have—should have—wakened the dead. For a kid who couldn't be three feet tall, she had the vocal range of an *American Idol* winner.

Abruptly, a woman charged out of the house, leaving the front door flapping open, making it pretty clear she feared her daughter was in imminent danger. Mike, of course, didn't know it was the kid's mother. But it seemed fairly obvious.

She had the same curly red hair. On her, it was a rich, dark auburn, dancing around her shoulders.

Unlike her daughter, she was wearing mostly green, but she had the same put-together thing going on. Her shirt was green and white, her jeans white, sandals green. Everything matched. The woman just had a few fewer sequins and rhinestones.

Mike took one quick look, but then had to do a double take.

That fast, he told himself it was a damned good thing he'd given up sex for the rest of his life. Redheads were trouble, every guy knew that. And undoubtedly she was married. Still, he'd have to be dead not to recognize she was beyond attractive. She was built lithe and long, lean like a runner, yet still had an upstairs rack compelling enough to glue his gaze there. The green eyes were gorgeous, the long face fine-boned and arresting. The mouth…man, that mouth, was not just luscious in shape but darned near riveting.

The whole package moved way past beautiful and into the stunning range.

Thankfully there was no time to dwell on it—both of them were distracted by all hell breaking loose. An elegant, long-haired pure-white kitten stepped out of the lady's open front door and promptly sat in the sun to delicately wash a paw.

Cat—the scarred-up old tomcat who'd shown up in a rainstorm a year ago and refused to leave him—suddenly shot out of the cat door and beelined for the kitten.

The mom promptly let out a shriek that verified forever where the daughter had inherited her vocal cords.

The kitten disappeared inside the open front door, followed by Cat. Both dogs, now that felines were in the picture, chased right in behind them. Teddy and the little girl pushed elbows, both trying to barrel after their respective pets.

Which left him—at least for a second—with the stranger.

She seemed to do a quick size up, which made Mike ultra conscious that he was shirtless, dirty and sweaty. But he couldn't tell from her expression what she thought of him. What she thought of the situation was more clear.

She was still gasping for breath. "I'm afraid we'll have to exchange names another time. I mean, I'd hoped to meet my neighbors under a little less chaotic condition—"

"Same here, believe me."

"Even though I'm tempted to cry right now, I have a feeling by tonight I'll be laughing about all this."

"Me, too." He liked it. That she wasn't turning hysterical—at least, once she'd realized her daughter wasn't hurt or in danger.

"Unfortunately…" Finally she caught her breath. "My cat hasn't been spayed yet. Neither has our dog. We hope to breed them."

"Uh-oh," Mike said, and that had to be the end of

the conversation. He hadn't run track since college, but in a crisis, he could always pour on the coals.

This definitely qualified as a pour-on-the-coals moment.

Amanda Scott sprinted right behind her new neighbor, calling for the kids, dogs and cats as loudly as he did. She'd had a moving company deliver the heavy boxes and furniture days before, but she hadn't planned on seriously moving in until today. Naturally, the house had a post-cyclone decor. Packing boxes and cartons and furniture were strewn every which way, creating obstacles that impeded their progress… but that wasn't the only reason she couldn't catch her breath.

It was him.

She'd known the transition from city life to the suburbs would be challenging, but she wasn't expecting *this* kind of challenging.

For five years, she'd lived her dream of a life—a gorgeous condo in downtown Chicago, an advertising job she thrived on and marriage to a perfect guy, Thom. Then came their precious baby. Then came the divorce.

The first thing she'd done—because it was the most critical issue—was give up sex for the rest of her life. Her inability to judge character in men was the reason, and Amanda was never one to duck from the truth. Although she'd moved to the suburbs solely for her daughter's sake, Amanda figured it'd work like a charm on the celibacy thing. After all, what males was she likely to run into but married men, dads and guys heavily into their families?

Her new neighbor was undoubtedly one of the married herd. She couldn't imagine any sane woman letting him run around loose and single. It was just…he was an unexpected jolt to her senses. Nothing unusual about the dark brown hair, but his chin had several days of disreputable unshaven whiskers. His brown eyes looked her over like a sip of warm Southern whiskey. The naked chest was smooth and sculpted; the jeans low-slung, his skin had a gleam of sun and sweat… The whole package wasn't just a prize male specimen. He was a whole bucket of testosterone.

He hollered again for his son, his dog, his cat. Even his voice had that guy-tenor thing going on.

It wasn't as if she was going to do anything about it. She'd just really hoped to have a little old lady for a neighbor. Or a family with a half dozen kids and a harried-looking father with a paunch.

Beyond the living area was the kitchen with its fresh birch cabinets and wonderful bay window—partly why she'd fallen in love with the house. Right now, boxes were stacked there every which way. The kitten was on top of one. Amanda saw her neighbor swoop up Princess—who immediately curled up on his shoulder as if she'd finally found her Prince Charming. Of course, she should be happy. He'd saved her from the tomcat prowling around the boxes for her.

"I'll take her," Amanda told him. He promptly handed her over in a cloud of white cat hair, and she quickly carted Princess to the nearest bathroom and closed the door.

One cat safe, now just two dogs and two kids to catch.

The dogs had quit barking—which struck Amanda as an ominous sign. The sound of crying was another bad sign—she wasn't sure which of their kids was unhappy, but the noise came from the second floor, where there were two bedrooms and a bath.

Amanda reacted to the crying first, took the stairs three at a time, and found her sweet, delicate daughter sitting on top of the neighbor boy, pretty much pounding on him. She was half his weight, but as Amanda knew, when her darling lost her temper, she seemed to gain the strength of Goliath. She pulled Molly off the boy, scolding her for hitting.

"Never hit," Amanda said firmly. "You know better. No one hits in our house. Ever. If you have an argument you can't solve, you come to me. But we don't hit. Apologize right now."

There followed a noisy dialogue of "But he…" and "She said it first…" and "No, it was him. I couldn't help it…" and "You were the one who was mean, mean and mean." Et cetera.

It took a few minutes to get the tears stopped, to

check both kids to make sure neither was actually hurt. The neighbor's boy looked just like his dad—rugged, pure male, a kid-adorable version of the grown-up.

Her new neighbor showed up at the top of the stairs. "I found the dogs."

"Where?"

"In the room I think is going to be your living room. Behind the couch. Slugger is now outside—I closed the front door, by the way, so we won't have any immediate repeat of this. And it's been fun, but I wouldn't want to overstay our welcome." He held out a hand, and his son immediately climbed up and did a stranglehold on his dad's neck. The other arm held his tomcat. Amanda could hear the hound baying and scratching at the front door from two stories up.

"Um..." She scratched her neck. How to end this impossibly awful first encounter? "Nice to meet you?"

"Actually we haven't met. Which is maybe a thank-God." He was already barreling down the stairs with both arms mighty full. His son was talking nonstop. The godforsaken cat was yowling in his other ear. "If you need help moving in, give a shout."

"Thanks," she said. She figured, after this, she'd ask him for help the day it rained money. "Same here."

His brows arched as if he couldn't imagine he'd need help from her or her household...yet his grin was still evident. A cheeky grin. A grin that said, "Hell, if you're going to have an awful day, might as well do it full bore."

An interesting man, she thought. The whole household looked slightly on the rascally side. The cat had more scars than a derelict. The dog had that hound smell, and its ears trailed the ground. All four of them could have used a bath and some clean clothes and a hairbrush.

But he could have yelled—the way most men did in a crisis. Or lost patience. Or made a point of finding blame, making it someone's fault—undoubtedly hers.

Instead, he'd just kind of charged in and started solving problems.

Maybe he wouldn't be such a terrible neighbor.

"Mom!" Molly tugged at her hand. "I don't want to see that boy again as long as I live! I hate him! And I'm thirsty! And I want to watch TV!"

Amanda almost laughed. For a few seconds there, she'd been worried about a personal connection to her neighbor. But her real life erased that worry lickety-split.

Right now she had all the chaos she could possibly handle—and then some.

Chapter Two

"I don't get it, Dad. Why she hit me. And did you see? I didn't hit her back."

"Yup, I saw, Teddy. You did the right thing. It's never okay for a boy to hit a girl. Or for someone to hit someone smaller than they are."

"But I wanted to. I wanted to *really, really* bad."

"Of course you did. She wasn't behaving well. But you just can't hurt another person. If you feel mad, you have to let it out other ways...like running as fast as you can for a while. Or punching a pillow. Or getting your mind off it by doing something else, something you like, like a puzzle or your trucks or something like that."

When Teddy stepped from the bathtub onto the

white-and-black-checked tile, Mike was waiting with a man-size black bath towel. Teddy might be squeaky-clean, but the bathroom now had more water than a lake. His son thought he was *way* big enough to take a bath alone. Maybe he was. But Mike wasn't sure the house could survive the aftermath. Even with him right there, everything in sight and vicinity tended to get soaked.

He covered Teddy's head, heard him giggle, swooped the damp package in his arms and carted him down the hall into the only room in the house that was decorated—seriously decorated.

The bed was shaped like a car. The wallpaper was a mass of trucks and cars and tractors. Mike had laid down thick, soft brown carpet, both to suck up extraneous noise and because four-year-olds—at least, his four-year-old—tended to accumulate bruises and bumps, so the carpet needed serious cushioning. No curtains. "We men," as Teddy put it, "don't need girl stuff like that."

Half the room was toys. Because Teddy's favorites tended to be moving vehicles, Mike had set him up with a "garage" for the diggers and tractors and haulers, and a couple of bins for the fifty million cars that reproduced every night. Mike had told him flat out that he didn't care—at all—about being tidy. But the cars had to be put away before bed, because Teddy could be hurt if he got up in the night to pee and stumbled over them.

Teddy considered that rule to be reasonable, which was a relief. When Teddy didn't like a rule, he could spend four hours asking "But, *why?*" questions to exhaust his father.

"I didn't say good night to the worms, Dad," Teddy suddenly worried.

"I'll say good night for you." Off went the towel. On went the football pj's.

"Why didn't she like me?"

"Who?" Silly question, Mike thought. It had to be the girl next door, from his son's mournful tone. "Maybe she did. Sometimes girls do strange things when they like a boy."

"I offered to show her my worms."

"That was very kind."

"We're going to dig in the backyard tomorrow, right, Dad? Make a big hole?"

"That's going to take some time to set up, sport. We'll be headed to the hardware store for supplies first. And Grandma and Grandpa want you to come over. But believe me, you and I are going to get into all the dirt and water and messes you could possibly want."

"I can't wait."

"We'll have fun," Mike promised him, and started the ritual tucking-in process.

"Dad?"

"What?"

"I bin thinking about why Mom doesn't want me

anymore. Maybe it's like that girl. Even when you're nice, some girls just don't like boys."

"Anyone who didn't like you would have to be really, really lame. And your mom loves you." Mike bent down, bussed his son's forehead. They weren't calling it a good-night kiss anymore. They were calling it a Night Connect.

"You're going to leave the bathroom light on?"

"Hey, it stays on 24/7. You know that."

Mike finally switched off the bedroom light and aimed for the living room. Teddy had barely said a word until he was three. Ever since then, he made up for it by talking every waking moment. Mike vaguely remembered working fourteen-hour days, poring over law books and briefs, skipping meals and sleep, never too tired to party.

To caretake a four-year-old all day—now *that* was tiring.

He grabbed a longneck from the fridge, the newspaper from the counter, sank into the easy chair by the window and propped up a foot.

He'd made the place as easy to care for as he could. Nothing in the living area but the big stone fireplace, a couch, a chair, the big TV. The open kitchen area had an eating nook, where you could see the TV whether you were eating or cooking. Mike had dibs on the west corner for his desk and computer and work setup. Teddy had dibs on the north corner, where he stashed his downstairs toys. Four-year-olds, Mike discovered, never seemed to have enough toys.

The silence now was more valued than gold. He didn't even get the paper opened before Slugger and Cat climbed up—Cat by his neck, Slugger taking up all available space on his lap. They promptly went into snooze mode.

The last of daylight blurred into sunset, and then true darkness came on. He never turned on a light. A full moon was just rising. He leaned his head back, taking a lazy moon bath in the open window. He scratched under Cat's chin, hearing him purr like thunder, and used the other hand to rub Slugger's belly, who loved that attention to the point of bliss.

He was just plain enjoying the simple evening, until his gaze accidentally glanced next door. Abruptly he stopped relaxing, stopped moving, stopped breathing.

Next door…in a second-story window…there appeared to be a navel. A naked navel.

Separating from the dog and cat, Mike climbed to his feet to take a clearer gander from the front picture window. Yup. There was a definitely a bare body in the window. Of course, he couldn't see the whole body—just the wedge between rib cage and midhip. Still, he could clearly see in the indentation of waist. The swell of curves over the hip. The belly button. An innie belly button.

Navels had never been his particular fantasy. He'd

always tended to be a leg man. And a breast man. And a fanny man. Hell, he'd always been a sex-crazed adolescent who'd turned into a wildly enthusiastic lover as an adult—until he'd recently given up sex, of course. But this was the first time he could recall ever noticing or being attracted to a belly button before.

What on earth was she doing?

Ah. Painting. He figured it out when she bent down—apparently from a ladder, because he could see her hand now holding a dripping brush. She pressed her belly against the window for support again, as she hand-painted the edge around the ceiling. Not that he could see the ceiling. But the dance back-and-forth motion of her arm pretty much told the story.

He told himself, okay, he'd figured it out, time to get away from the window. She might catch him being a navel voyeur. Worse yet, the longer he stared, the more he started worrying that maybe he really was a navel voyeur. Or that he could turn into one.

He was about to turn away except that he suddenly saw a blur of movement. Even with windows open in both places, he heard only a vague sound coming from the second story in her place, but something had obviously happened. She suddenly disappeared from the window. So did the ladder.

He didn't *know* she fell.

But there was suddenly no sign of life or movement

up there. And a fall from a ladder could be darned serious.

He couldn't leave his son, of course. He never left his son alone. Teddy had occasional nightmares, besides. Still…how long could a quick check take?

He didn't even bother with shoes, just sprinted out the front door, already calling himself every flavor of dumb. She undoubtedly locked the house, so he wouldn't be able to get in…but it was open, he discovered when he turned the knob on her front porch. Where was her head? A woman and little girl alone in the house after dark, and she hadn't locked the door?

He considered knocking, but was afraid he'd rouse the prissy white dog into a fit of barking that would waken her daughter. He just called quietly, "Hey…it's me from next door. Mike. I was in my living room, thought I saw you fall from upstairs. I'm not trying to be nosy. I'll go right back home. I just wanted to make sure—"

Abruptly he quit with the bumbling greeting. Even from her living-room foyer, he heard a groan coming from the second story.

He vaulted upstairs, had no problem identifying which room she was in, because night-lights reflected in the bathroom and kid's room. It was the room with the ceiling light shining in the hallway where the redhead had to be.

He pelted in, took in the mess at a glance—the

wobbly ladder on its side. The newspapers spread over the painting area, with the usual gambit of brushes and rollers and blue tape and supplies. It wasn't hard to tell what color she was painting the room, because there was now baby-blue all over her, the floor, the walls and everything else.

He didn't give a damn about the spilled paint. She was lying in the middle of it. He knelt down, fast, and saw with relief that her eyes were open—even if they did look dazed.

"Don't move," he said.

"Are you kidding? I couldn't move if I tried."

"At least you're talking. And I don't see any blood." He just saw a whole lot of baby blue. In her hair. On her chin. On her halter top. On her tummy. On her shorts. On the floor, too, but the gleam of baby blue on the floor wasn't interesting. "Where does it hurt the worst?"

"How am I going to get this out of my hair?"

"How about if we worry if you need an ambulance before we let vanity into the picture?"

"It's not vanity that's killing me. It's pride. I *just* bought that stupid ladder!"

He'd already noticed the pip-squeak–quality ladder. "You bought a girl ladder. Instead of a sturdy, practical one."

"I couldn't carry the sturdy ones! They were too heavy! Besides, it wasn't the ladder that caused the fall. At least, not exactly. My mom called. If you knew my parents, you'd understand why I fell."

It was pretty obvious that the fall had unleashed her ditsy side, because she started babbling nonstop. While she ranted on, he looked her over more seriously. Obviously her head and spine would be the most serious worries, after a crash like that, but she could also have broken or sprained something. He started by examining her feet—which were bare except for the neon-painted tocnails.

"My parents are wonderful. Both of them. It's just that they raised me to be spoiled. To believe that I deserved everything, from Prince Charming to a perfect life. You have no idea how useless I am."

"Uh-huh." The calves were perfect. No fat. Just those perfect curves, leading to delectably soft thighs.

"My mom—her name is Gretchen—she wanted to hire painters for me. And a decorator for the house. And to pay for a summer program for precocious four-year-olds."

He figured, since she was conscious if not exactly lucid, that he'd better keep his hands off her belly and breasts. Technically he supposed he should check things like ribs and all. But since he was already mightily turned on—against his will—he knew perfectly well that the wrong kind of touching was on his mind. He'd lost all interest in checking for injuries.

Still, he tried to get his attention back on track. Her

neck was fair game. Shoulders. Hands. Wrists. And she'd stopped talking—for the few seconds it took to carefully and touch and probe those areas—he followed through with a question. "So what did you tell your mother when she wanted to do all those things for you?"

"I told her—*and* my dad—that Molly and I moved closer specifically so they had a chance to be more active grandparents. I know they wanted more time with Molly. And I wanted that, too, for it to be easier for them to be a regular part of her life. But I also told them I didn't want anything else."

"And this was a problem somehow?"

"Hey." Apparently she forgot the conversational track. Her fingers suddenly banded his wrist, and her gaze met his, clear as daylight. "Quit right there. No touching below the neck. For Pete's sake, we haven't even been introduced."

"I'm Mike Conroy."

"I'm Amanda Scott." There was humor in her eyes now. He *had* introduced himself quickly. "I can get up. I'm pretty sure."

"Let's do it slowly."

"You know, I would *really* like to stop meeting like this. We could try it all over again. You know. Behave like real neighbors. Knock on the door. Show up with cookies or a beer or a bottle of wine. Say hi, welcome to the neighborhood. I mean, we could try meeting without a disaster. Oh, no, no, Darling!"

Startled, Mike couldn't fathom where the endearment came from—but then he realized the half-breed white dog had shown up, clearly realizing something was wrong with her mistress. She was aiming straight for the puddle of paint on the floor.

"Got it," Mike said, and lurched for the dog. The poodle or poodle mix—whatever the devil she was—didn't object to being hauled up in the air. She seemed to expect being carried. He suspected going home would entail Slugger giving him hell—and howls—if he showed up smelling like girl-poodle, but there was no help for it.

"Could you put her in Molly's room, and then just close the door without latching it? She loves sleeping with Molly."

"Got it. Only, you don't try standing up until I get back."

A night-light was the only illumination in the girl's room, but Mike could readily make out that it was a girl's version of what he'd done for Teddy. Amanda, though, had gone even more overboard. Shelves were jammed with stuffed animals. A bitsy dressing table had a matching bitsy chair. The kid was swallowed somewhere in a canopy bed, and it was hard to find a path to walk between the flounces and little chairs and dolls. *Lots* of dolls. Dolls in cradles, dolls in various states of undress, dolls on shelves, dolls on the floor, dolls without heads.

Finally he located the little doll—the real one—on

the pillows under the canopy deal. The rosebud mouth was emitting a few teensy snores. The red hair curled all over the pillow. She'd kicked off half the covers. Mike set the poodle down, who promptly circled and settled at the foot of the bed, then tugged up the covers. He discovered a clearly sacred blankie had fallen on the carpet, and retrieved it. He knew about sacred blankies. Anyway. The kid was fine. The dog was fine.

But on returning to the empty room next door, he discovered that Amanda wasn't remotely fine.

She'd made it to a sitting position. Was sitting with her knees up, one hand on her forehead, making choking sounds as if she were holding back tears...only, tears were flooding her eyes in thick clear drips, turning her pearl-cream skin blotchy, turning... Aw, hell, she wasn't just a mess. She was a complete mess.

"Something hurts that bad?" He crouched down.

"Go away. Thank you for helping. But go away. I'm fine."

Yeah, he knew that female twist. No matter what he did now, he'd be in trouble. She wasn't fine. But she didn't want him here—and he sure as hell didn't want to be here. But he sure as hell couldn't leave a woman crying her eyes out.

"I'll tell you what," he started to say.

"No. I mean it. I'm fine. I'm just having a melt-down. People have meltdowns. I'll get over it. But

I really don't want to do this in front of a stranger, okay? So just go away."

"I will, I will. But here's the thing. What if you have a concussion?"

"I don't."

"It looked as if you fell partly on the side of your head, because I felt quite a bump—"

"I don't care."

He squinted, scratched his nape, thinking that was another female comment that was invariably booby-trapped. Obviously she had to care if she had a concussion, if she needed medical attention—for her daughter's sake, if not for her own. She wanted him to disappear. He got it. But if he went back to his place, he wasn't going to sleep all night, worrying whether she'd collapsed over here alone.

"I've got a plan," he said firmly. "You head into the shower. Clean up. Get the paint out of your hair and all that. And I'll be downstairs. Nowhere near you. You come out of the shower, call down that you're all right, then I'll lock your door and go home."

She was still sniffling hard, but she let loose an almost inaudible "All right. Only because I'm worried about Molly."

"Got it." He didn't care why she agreed. She agreed. He helped her stand up, trying to think like a big brother, not an adult man who was handling attractive female flesh, but it wasn't that simple. When a woman was vulnerable, a guy instinctively reacted.

It was a sick instinct, a stupid instinct, an instinct that got a guy in trouble every time, but whatever. The brush of her body against his provoked an unfortunately magnificent hard-on. He'd just touched her side, her arm, her hair… That was all it took. Some baby-blue paint came off in his hand when he touched her hair…which she saw.

"It's just latex," he assured her. "It'll come out with plain old soap and water."

It seemed an innocent enough comment to him, but, par for the course, he must have picked just the wrong thing to say, because her eyes welled up all over again. Still, she stumbled off, disappearing into master bath right off her bedroom, and closed the door.

That left him staring at her mess. It wasn't his problem, of course. And he'd the same as promised her that he was going downstairs, away from her personal space. But it really *was* a mess. It wasn't just the overturned paint can, but the wet brush lying on the floor, the overturned ladder, the roller and pan still soaked with that same sissy-blue color.

If she had to come out of a fresh shower and clean all this up…well, he could just picture her breaking into tears all over again.

It's not as if that was his problem, either, but he was stuck hanging around until she came out of the shower. She could still fall. She could still have a concussion. He wasn't about to leave Teddy alone next door much longer, but he was probably committed for another ten minutes anyway.

So he started to clean up…except that when he picked up the paintbrush and actually looked at the project—well, she had only a couple of square feet to go near the ceiling. It was downright silly to seal up and clean up, when just that little bit was left to do.

He finished the bit of wall in two shakes. She still wasn't out of the shower—he could hear the water running from beyond the closed door. She was making noise—some might call it a frightening attempt at singing the blues—but the noise at least verified that she hadn't keeled over.

He'd just do a little more cleanup. And then split.

Amanda couldn't *believe* it took so long to wash off all the paint.

She shampooed and soaked and shampooed all over again. She scrubbed her skin practically raw, then conditioned and rinsed and soaked some more.

Eventually she had to climb out. She just didn't want to. She wanted to stay holed up in the bathroom until her neighbor was gone for sure. How humiliating, to have a meltdown in front of him. She was a crybaby. Always had been, always would be.

But she'd hoped her hunky neighbor would never have to know that.

She toweled off, pulled on a clean T-shirt and shorts, opened the door a peek to let out the steam—and to listen. No sounds. She'd have heard Molly—she'd been known to hear her baby from two floors away from behind closed doors. But in this case, she only listened for the clump of a heavy footstep, a tenor sigh…the hint of testosterone in the air.

Nothing.

Still rubbing the towel through her hair, she tiptoed across the hall to her bedroom…or her bedroom-to-be. Until the room got painted and carpet was put in, she'd been camping on a couch. The point, though, was that Mike was definitely gone.

But so was her disaster area. The paint can, newspapers, roller and pan, brushes—everything had disappeared. He'd finished painting the rest of the wall. A few splotches of "Clear Skies" blue still marred the floor, but there was nothing else in the room—except for a note.

"I stole your ladder—so you wouldn't use it again. Mine's hanging in the garage. Borrow it anytime you want. I'll have your painting supplies back on your porch by tomorrow—it was just easier to clean up in my basement than mess up your new place."

There was no signature, no personal comment. He'd just come to her rescue out of the complete blue. Did the whole silent take-care-of thing.

She flipped off the overhead light, stalked over

to the window—carefully avoiding the splotches of paint—and stared down at his place.

There were no lights on that she could see. No dangerously good-looking adult male in sight. But he was going to be a problem, she could just smell it.

All her life she'd needed a hero.

Except for now. Right now she needed to stand on her own—to learn to stand on her own—or die trying. She was running out of chances to feel proud of herself and her life. The suburbs was it. Her foxhole in the battle. Her line in the sand. Her Custer's last stand.

She wasn't going to *need* a man. Ever again.

Chapter Three

The next morning, keeping his eye on the time, Mike clattered down the basement steps just ahead of his son. Teddy was running in circles—even on the stairs—chanting, "Hoboy, hoboy, hoboy!"

His joy, naturally, was about the worm-farm project. And before Teddy had woken up, Mike had hustled downstairs to set it up. The "ingredients" needed for the farm were all laid out—the plastic drawers, newspaper, garbage, burlap and, of course, the worms.

"Now, both of us have jobs," he told his son. "Your job is to tear up the newspaper. Like this. That's to make the bed for the worms."

Teddy took to ripping up paper like a nun took to

prayer. "I'm doing this really, really good, aren't I, Dad?"

"You sure are. And then…we're going to add just a little water. That'll be my job." Mike wasn't born yesterday. A "little water" to his son was like inviting Armageddon. "But you get to do the next thing. The worms need food. Something we call 'organic waste.'"

"What's that?"

"Organic waste is the stuff we usually put down the disposal. Like old lettuce. Maybe some carrots and carrot stalks. We could try a little broccoli."

"Dad," Teddy said earnestly. "I think we should give the worms all the broccoli in the whole world."

"That's precisely how I feel about brussels sprouts. Okay. Now…we add the worms."

"Can I do that? Can I? Can I?"

"Are you kidding? The worms are *totally* your job."

"Thanks, Dad!" The thrill on his son's face was almost as good as Christmas.

Finally, the project was finished, and Mike could put the lid on. "Okay. Your grandma's coming in fifteen or twenty minutes, so we've got just enough time to get you cleaned up. But remember, we can't look at the worms for at least two weeks."

"Except for peeks."

"No. No exceptions. No peeks. No looking at all. Light can hurt them. Okay? Promise."

"I promise with my whole life. I promise, hope to die."

While Mike was dunking Teddy in the tub and then getting him brushed and dressed, he took advantage to give his son the bigger worm picture. "Even though we have to wait two weeks to see the worms again, we have lots of good things to do in the meantime. Like building our water garden in the backyard."

"For the frogs." Teddy lifted his hands so Mike could thread a fresh T-shirt over his head.

"Yeah, for the frogs. The frogs are going to love those worms. And there'll be extra worms for fishing. And we can even use the worms' waste besides that."

"What waste?"

"Their castings and tea." Mike should have known his son wouldn't let him off that easy. "That's their poop and urine. It works like a fertilizer. So we can dump that in another part of the yard, like where we plant bushes or trees… Hey, I hear the doorbell. That'll be your Grandma Conroy."

"No! Do I *have* to go, Dad? I want to stay with you."

His parents may have been unhappy about the divorce, but both were thrilled to have their one and only grandson suddenly within three miles of them. Barbara Conroy had always tended to dress on the formal side, but today she wore snug jeans and a long T-shirt—a perfect getup for surviving the day with a four-year-old. "Hey, you." She snagged a kiss off him first, gave him a motherly look over. "You doing okay?"

"Couldn't be better."

She said something to him—but his attention was diverted when a car pulled up next door. It was a meeting of the Lexuses. His mom's was lipstick-red, Amanda's mom favored a custom-painted sapphirc. Apparently it was a mutual grandma-pick-up-grandkid day.

Both grandmothers looked alike—blondish hair, great bones, slim and both appearing energetic and younger than their years. They spotted each other, about the same time Molly skipped out the door and saw Teddy.

Molly stuck out her tongue at Teddy. The insult was returned. Then Slugger started baying because the poodle next door started an excited-barking thing. The grandmothers started talking and laughing at the commotion, but for one whole, long second, all he saw was her.

Amanda.

The grandmas herded their respective grandkids into their respective Lexuses. Mike heard Amanda tell her mother, "Mom, please don't call her prin-cess" and then a minute later, "Mom, no buying her a million toys. Just be together, okay? Have a good time."

And her mom responded with a chant of "uh-huh, uh-huh" as if they'd had this conversation a zillion times before, and the whole while she was winking at her granddaughter. Molly appeared to need several suitcases to be gone for a few hours.

Teddy just galloped to the car and climbed in. By the time the cars pulled out and all the noise disappeared—even the dogs quieted down—suddenly there were just the two of them with nothing more than a spare stretch of driveway separating them.

Lightning arced between them, even though there wasn't a single cloud in the sky.

"I owe you a big thanks," she called out.

"No sweat." He'd put her painting stuff on the back porch before daybreak, hoping he wouldn't have to run into her. But now, the more he looked at her, the more he relaxed. Last night, there'd been something… off…between them. An intimacy, because of being alone at night, the dark, her not wearing much and then nothing while she was in the shower, her crying, the whole thing.

It wasn't as if that chemical-lightning thing had disappeared. If anything, the charge was more intense—but now he was braced for it. And looking at her this morning was reassuring. She looked… well…prissy. Not vulnerable and cute, like last night, with the naked navel and the wild heap of red hair.

Today, her hair was scooped up, a spotless yellow shirt paired with white shorts, sandals with yellow flowers. And she had on makeup. At this hour of the morning.

He hadn't shaved in three days now—hadn't brushed his hair in two. No reason to spruce up—he wasn't trying to please or attract any female again. Still, he was glad to admit he had a heap of things he had to do—she hastily admitted the same—and they both took off in opposite directions.

It was the truth, besides, Mike thought self-righteously. With Teddy gone, it was a perfect chance to make a trip to the hardware store.

Amanda let Darling out for a quick business trip in the backyard, petted Princess, grabbed her car keys and list and headed out. She'd had a spiffy Austin Healey before the divorce. Now she had a white SUV, which looked like a clone of all the soccer moms' transport vehicles up and down the neighborhood.

Mike was gone, she noticed. At least, his garage door was open and his truck nowhere in sight. She hadn't forgotten what a hero he'd been for her last night, but thankfully, she'd wakened this morning certain that he was a resistible hero. They both had their hands full with major life changes right now. And she wasn't about to forget the major life lesson that had been battered into her by the divorce.

She wasn't going to be the needy one in a relationship ever again.

She backed out of the drive and turned left—then immediately realized she should have steered right. It was going to take a while before she got her bearings in the neighborhood, and hardware stores were hardly her normal milieu. This morning, though, she had a major hardware-store type of list. She wanted bricks, to make a brick walkway in the back. Mulch. Stones. Eventually she wanted a porch swing back there, too.

In the meantime, she needed just *stuff*. Gardening gloves. A little spade. A little shovel. She didn't even have a flashlight in the house. Somehow she had to figure out a way to mow the grass. And Mike—not that she wanted to keep dwelling on her neighbor— had intimated she needed a sturdier ladder.

She located the store—after only a couple of wrong turns—and even found a reasonably close parking spot. She'd been in one of these warehouse hardware stores before. Once. But she didn't have a clue where anything was, so she just grabbed a cart and pulled out her list. She figured she'd get the boring stuff over with first—the household tools. Hammers and screwdrivers and flashlights. Picture-hanger doohickeys. Things like that.

Thankfully that chore didn't take long, but once she wandered into the garden center, there seemed a million choices, a million things to look at. She slowed down. Absently started humming...

Moments later, she realized someone else was humming, too. A man's hum. Not in the same aisle where she was looking at bricks and stones, but somewhere not far. When she stopped humming to listen, he stopped, too.

When she started humming again, so did he.

She glanced around the corner into the next aisle. Saw nothing. Shaking her head, she continued on. She would have to find some help, get someone to carry the bulky items for her. In the meantime...well, she wasn't sure how she ended up in the plumbing aisle, but suddenly there he was.

Mike.

He spotted her about the same time she spotted him. He had a faucet set in his hand. She was still holding her list. But for a petrifying second, she forgot what she was doing altogether.

She told herself swiftly that it was nothing like the night before. Granted, he'd come across as this handsome, wonderful white knight, all sexy eyes and protectiveness and strength...but she so wasn't about to believe in the fairy-tale thing again.

And once she caught her breath, she realized it was okay today. Better. He was just an oversized scruffy mutt, after all. And as long as she didn't look directly in his eyes, she didn't feel any of those...well, zingers. As if she'd been prodded with something electric and compelling. As if she was somehow meant to move closer to him.

She tried a light laugh. "I swear, we keep meeting in the oddest places!"

He finally looked away from her, too, and lifted the package in his hands. "I've been looking at faucets. Nothing exactly wrong with what we've got, but there's a new kind..." He showed her. "You can turn it on and off with a wrist, never have to touch a handle. Which means that little boys—and big ones—don't necessarily have to wipe out a whole sink when they're cleaning up."

"Now that would be a miracle," she said with another laugh, this one more natural. "I'm new at the yard-and-gardening business. Never had any 'green' to work with in the city. So I've just been shopping for some general tools and landscaping stuff."

"Yeah, we're getting into that kind of trouble in our house, too."

So much for small talk. She took a breath, knowing she really needed some things to be said. "Look. I can't thank you enough for last night. You certainly didn't need to finish painting the wall or doing the cleanup—that was way over the top. And after I cried all over you, too."

"Yeah, that was really awful. Don't do it again."

She was startled, then realized he was teasing. His crook of a smile momentarily disarmed her, but then, blast it, she realized she was looking at him again, feeling the pull of, say, an earthquake or a tsunami.

"Well, I owe you a payback." She hoped her voice came out sounding normal.

"Forget it. No problem."

"I was thinking of bringing you a homemade lasagna—"

"Whoa. Complete change of mind. You *do* owe me a payback."

This time they both laughed. "So you like lasagna. Okay. Done deal. I'll bring it over tomorrow, around 5:00 p.m. or so." She pulled her cart, as if she were going to go back to her shopping, but then couldn't seem to resist asking, "Was that your mom who picked up Teddy?"

"Yeah. Barbara. And my dad's name is David. They're over the moon we bought the house here. Teddy's the first grandchild. Their place is just a few towns over, in Lisle."

She pulled at her cart again, as if she had the good sense to cut the small talk and go back to her shopping chores. Somehow, her feet seemed rooted right there, temporarily, though. She couldn't seem to quell a second round of nosiness. "How about Teddy's mom?" When Mike lifted an eyebrow, she said swiftly, "I know, I know. It's none of my business. But if we're living next door, I don't want to accidentally say something hurtful or difficult for your son, so... you know."

"Yeah, I know." His arched brow suggested he knew perfectly well she was being nosy. But he answered. "Right now I've got primary physical custody. My ex-wife hasn't remarried yet, but she's about to be." He lowered the brow. "Truth is, Teddy's real bent out of shape about his mother. He doesn't get it. Why his mom would take off. He seems to believe that she personally abandoned him."

Amanda shot him a sympathetic look. "I'm sorry."

"I didn't tell you to solicit sympathy. But it's like you said—if we're living so close, we should probably know what the situation is with our kids."

She nodded, and immediately came through with her stash of baggage. "My ex is Thom. He has regular visitation rights, although he only makes it half the time. I had a job in advertising—we lived downtown Chicago—but after the divorce… Well, Molly's about to start preschool, so I figured it was time to move to the suburbs, settle where there were good schools and families and other kids for Molly to play with." She added wryly, "To be honest, I'm finding the move a little bit of a culture shock."

"Hey, you're not alone. I never envisioned living in suburbia, either. But I felt the same, for Teddy's sake. Wanted the kind of neighborhood where he could grow up, go out and play, meet other kids, do the good-school thing. And the clincher for me was living closer to his grandparents." Abruptly he straightened, as if he feeling he'd shared too much. Or that he'd found too much in common with her. "Well, I'd better—"

"Me, too," she said instantly, and did a quick U-turn with the cart. "I need to move on. Just remember, lasagna tomorrow. If you're not there at five, I'll just leave it on the front porch. See you later."

She couldn't seem to escape the store that fast, though. She just seemed to need so much *stuff*. The weight kept adding up, for the bricks, the mulch, the stone. And once she hooked on to one of the store's employees, she asked for his help picking out a lawn mower. All the bulky and heavy stuff had to be delivered; there was just no way she could get it in and out of her car.

By the time she edged into the checkout line, her cart was full, and she was daydreaming about some lunch and a nap. As she reached down for her purse, though, she noticed something odd. The items she'd chosen had somehow changed. Somehow, the pink gardening gloves she'd chosen had metamorphosed into a heavier, ugly gray pair. The pretty little spade she'd picked out had turned into a set of gardening tools with sturdy steel handles. Instead of one shovel, there was now both a pointy shovel and a flat blade, neither particularly huge, but definitely sturdier than what she'd originally picked up.

For a second, she thought she had the wrong cart, but there were so many other things that she recognized—like the matching dishtowels and the porcelain drawer pulls and the shoe organizers and the picture-hanger doohickeys. She glanced behind her, around her. Mike was nowhere in sight. He'd undoubtedly long finished his shopping before she did.

But he was the only soul in the universe—at least, that she could imagine—who would have done this to her.

He couldn't keep pulling this white-knight thing on her.

This time, there would have to be serious pay-back.

Mike should have known that putting in the new faucet would turn into a federal project. Bad plumbing always led to more bad plumbing, even in a new place. Conceivably, the work was hampered by his being a *lot* better lawyer than he was a handyman. And by the dog, who wanted to sleep on his foot while he was lying on his back under the kitchen sink. And by Cat, who crawled up his leg and sat purring on his damned stomach while he was trying to wrench in the new connection.

Several phone calls interrupted him, adding more complications to the sweat-fest chore. The first call, he jumped for—hit his head, then his elbow. But it was Teddy. "Hey, Dad. Grandma said to tell you I'm being good and she wants me to stay overnight."

Mike could hear the tiny wobble in his son's voice. Teddy wasn't comfortable, being away from him at night. At least for now. "Not overnight, sport. I want you home. But if grandma wants you to stay for dinner, you can."

His son ran off, then called back three minutes later. "Okay. I'm having dinner here. Grandma says do you want to come?"

"Tell her no, thank you. But call me again if you'll be later than 7:30 p.m., okay?"

"Yeah. Grandma says she's gonna get me my own cell phone."

"No, she's not…" Mike shook his head. The connection was severed. There were possibly going to be a few complications, living this close to grandparents. Four years old? A cell phone? Not.

The other two calls he let go to the answering machine. Working with water and grease and heat under the sink was a whole lot more fun than talking to his ex. Nancy wanted to arrange a time to be with Teddy.

He'd call her back.

When he got around to it.

Even hearing her voice put a snarl in his mood. He was long over Nancy, but still testy on some of the divorce details. He was working on moving on, getting past it, all those stupid slogan words that divorced people used. But it was one thing to have a failed marriage…another to have your marriage end because your wife took off with a germ-freak nerd who couldn't weigh more than one hundred and fifty pounds.

That she could desire such a jerk was part of what festered. Even if the marriage had long lost its luster before the divorce, Mike never had any reason to doubt his ex was happy in bed. It wasn't losing her that hurt. It was losing her to such a ninny. His sexual pride still felt stomped on by a bulldozer.

Anyway. He'd had enough of chores by four o'clock. He showered, put on old shorts and his Harvard tee—his favorite, as exhibited by the frayed neck and holes—called the hound and aimed for the deck. Teddy wouldn't be home for a couple of hours. He figured a half hour of slouch time in the shade was just what the doctor ordered.

He opened the door to the deck—and almost tripped over a twelve pack of beer. Cold beer. Dripping, sweating cold. A fancy longneck brand. Bottles.

It was enough to make a warrior weep. Since he only hit a grocery store when he was desperate—those places were terrifying—he hadn't picked up beer or any other side goodies. He glanced around for a note, but he already knew who'd done this to him—even before he turned his head.

One glance was all it took to identify the slim, bare foot perched on the white lawn chair next door.

Her deck was smaller than his, with a lattice

privacy half wall—which was why he couldn't see the rest of her body. But he could see the foot. And the curve of her white calf.

The Sissy Dog was snoozing on her lap, but as if sensing testosterone in the air, she jumped to the ground and sat at the edge of the deck. Slugger was too tired to move—his position on life, twenty-three hours out of twenty-four—but his tail started wagging like a metronome.

Mike ignored the critters. He could hear Amanda talking on a cell phone, even if he couldn't see it. He opened a beer. He didn't want or mean to listen. He just figured he'd hang for a few moments so he could thank her once she finished her call. Except, she kept talking.

"Mom. Come on now. You know I love you, and I didn't mean to hurt your feelings. I'm just asking you not to call her princess… Yes, I *know* the kitten's name is Princess, but that's entirely different—Molly named her, and I couldn't talk her out of it. Mom…"

The foot lifted. Disappeared from sight. He heard the clunk of a glass, as if she'd poured something and then set the glass down on a metal surface.

"I *know* you called me princess. And you were a wonderful mom. The best. Dad was a wonderful dad. The best. But you two spoiled me rotten. I really want to raise Molly more independent than I was. I don't want her expecting…"

The foot showed up moments later with sex-red color on some of the toes. So. She was drinking, talking to her mother and repainting her toenails all at the same time. Obviously she came from the estrogen side of the species.

"…I didn't mean that, Mom. I'm just saying…I don't have skills. Skills I need. Skills I want. I don't know how to mow a lawn. How to shampoo a carpet. How to do anything *practical*. I knew how to behave at a cotillion, a country-club dance, a symphony. But I never saw Thom coming. He bamboozled me. I should have been too old to be bamboozled. He was cheating right in front of my eyes, and I never noticed the clues. *Mom.* I *know* I'm not stupid. But just because I was smart in school doesn't mean anything now. I need to be smart in life, and I'm a dimwit!"

The left foot was done, raised to be examined, then the right foot was started on. She was drinking wine, he identified, when a bottle showed up on the deck floor.

"No, no. I *love* how you raised me. I had the most wonderful childhood a girl could have. I'm just saying that times are a little different. I want Molly to be more self-reliant. To not expect a prince to rescue her, or to think she *needs* a prince to be happy. I want her to be able to rescue herself. No, no, I swear, I didn't mean it that way…*Mom*…all right! All right! I give up! You can pay for the riding lessons! But no buying her a horse! And I mean it!"

It seemed possible the phone call rather abruptly ended, because there was suddenly a series of muttered swear words from the other side of the lattice, all said in a tone of utter exhaustion. He finally had a chance to speak and he took it.

"Hey. Thanks for the beer."

There was a moment of total silence, and then a face showed up from the other side of the lattice. She wasn't completely naked, contrary to what his imagination had tried to lead him to believe. Her T-shirt read *Duke*. Maybe it was hers, maybe an old boyfriend's, but whichever, it was even older than his, more frayed, more holey. He gained respect for her right then and there. Of course, he also noticed the shortest shorts he'd ever seen. My God, she might be a redhead, but she did have a set of legs. En route, he did happen to glimpse she was shooting fire from her eyes.

"Were you *listening* to that conversation?"

"Me? I don't know what you mean. I just walked out on the deck a second ago, saw the beer, couldn't imagine anyone who would have left it but you. Appreciate it. Want one?"

"No, of course not. I... Yes."

He was going to have to rename her the whirling dervish. She put the Sissy Dog inside, grabbed her icer and wine bottle, her wineglass, and zipped down the steps and into his yard faster than he could retract the offer.

Slugger took one look and rolled on his back, assuming she'd want to pet him. She did. Then poured another glass of wine for herself. "I started with wine, so I don't want to mix it with beer, but I'm more than up for sharing a drink." She took the chair across from him—another Adirondack chair, nothing fancy. Her Duke T-shirt was so oversized that when she bent down again to rub Slugger's tummy, he could see the tips of a lace bra. The view suggested that there was a lot more bra than boob in there. The red toenails shined like Chinese lacquer. Her hair was swooped up, all messy, all wild, held off her neck with some clips.

It was hard to define why he liked the whole package. But he did.

A lot.

"What do you think?" She motioned to the space between their houses. "Do we need a fence? Because of the dogs and kids and all? I like the open space between the properties…but I don't know. A fence still seems like a good idea. At least if you think so. The point is that we should agree on the nature of fence, don't you think? And just for the record, I know perfectly well that it was you who sneaked the tools in my cart this morning."

He was having trouble following her fast changes in subject. Particularly when his attention was so zealously focused on her bare legs and inadequate neckline. "There was no point in your throwing away money on tools that weren't going to hold up. As far as I could tell, you weren't worried about price. You were just choosing stuff that had pink handles."

"Well, yes."

He wiped a hand over his face. No point in discussing that any further. "If you want a fence between the yards, naturally, I'll spring for my half."

"I'm not trying to be difficult. It was just an idea. If we both wanted a fence...I just didn't want to act unilaterally. For one thing, there are all kinds and types of fences—"

"I get it. You're not being difficult." She was. He wasn't sure why. He wasn't sure why they were talking about fences, either, except for the obvious reason. They wanted protection from each other.

"I've just had a really long day."

He thought she was trying to explain why she was being difficult again, but then he heard the old song "I Will Survive," and realized it was her designated cell-phone ring. She lifted a hand and, apologizing to him, said, "This'll be short, but I really need to take it."

"No sweat." He took another pull on his beer, put his bare feet on the deck rail and let his head fall back. In two seconds, he realized the caller was her ex-husband.

"I wasn't ducking your calls, Thom. We were busy with the move this week." And then, "I think it's a little ridiculous that you're pushing for equal custody when you couldn't even make the last two visitations. This isn't about Molly, and you know it. You just want the child support cut. It's not as if you can't afford it, for heaven's sake—"

She bounced up from the chair, turned her back—as if turning around would make it harder for Mike to hear her. Not.

"I'm not listening to yelling, Thom. Not now. Not ever. I expect you to pick her up on Saturday at noon. Have her back here by seven. I have nothing else to say."

Once she snapped the phone closed, she whirled around, her smile brighter than glass. "I'd turn off the cell phone but I can't. There could always be a call related to Molly."

"Same problem here. I can duck calls with the answering machine, but I don't want Teddy to have any problem getting hold of me." He felt a sudden restlessness. The kind of thing he felt when he was about to do something he shouldn't. She sashayed back to the chair, crossed her legs, all her movements classy and elegant—not a put-on, just apparently how she always was. The call from her ex should have been another turnoff. She was complicated, and so was her life and problems. Every encounter he'd had with her so far indicated she was high-maintenance, trouble, no one and nothing that he could possibly want in his life.

But damn it. She was so upset her hands were shaking.

She noticed him looking at her hands, and immediately said, "It's no secret to anyone. I hate confrontations. I'm terrible at them. My job used to be in advertising. Everybody called me tough. I *was* tough, I swear. But that was my business life. In my private life, well, you could say I flunked the course in fighting altogether."

"Amanda—?"

"What? Oh. I know. I'm talking too much. I pretty much don't drink at all for just that reason. One glass of wine and out it all spills. My life. And this was such a trying day—"

"And you're nervous around me."

"—and I'm nervous around you." She blinked. "I'm not. I don't know where that came from."

He hunched forward, motioned her closer.

She hunched forward with a curious frown.

He said, "Here's the thing. I've got one priority for this summer. Teddy. To get him set up. To make this a home. Check out the preschools and pediatricians. Find some kids in the neighborhood, locate the parks, the library, the stuff he can get involved in. That's my whole job this summer. And there just can't be any women in that picture."

"Okay."

"He's still ripped about the divorce. Sometimes I think it's because he never saw his mother and I argue. We never did, not in front of him. I thought that was how you were supposed to behave, but now—crazy as it sounds—I think it's part of the problem. He's got it in his head that Nancy left because of not wanting him, that he was somehow at fault. What Nancy pulled was a downright turkey move. But I can't change that or fix it. All I can do is try to settle my kid into the happiest, most stable life I can. To put it in blunt terms—"

"Do," she encouraged him.

"I've given up sex forever. Now it has occurred to me, in the past couple of days, that 'forever' might not be a precisely achievable goal. But through this summer, I really need to do the celibate thing. No entanglements. No distractions. My world has to be my kid."

"Whew!" She let out a long breath, tossed him a smile—not that glassy, classy smile but one so real it jammed the air in his lungs. It was that sexy. That natural. "You have no idea how glad I am to hear you say that. Mike—I'm in exactly the same boat."

"Yeah?"

"We're on the same page. I just made the no-sex vow the same way." She laughed, inviting him to. "The best thing about the divorce was figuring out how many wrong roads I'd been taking. I had every advantage a girl could have, was pampered and spoiled from the get-go, fell for the whole fairy tale that I was something special. I could have had a sign on my forehead that said Me-Me-Me."

"That sounds pretty harsh."

"It's the total truth. I thought my ex was the Prince Charming in the story. Never once looked further than the surface—until it all crashed. So…I'll likely look for a job in the fall. I don't know what kind. I'll work that out after Molly starts preschool. But I'm determined that this summer be about her. I want her to be about everything that I'm not. More self-reliant. More capable. I want her to take more pleasure in accomplishments than in material things. Which means…"

"Somehow I sense the punch line is coming."

"Yes. No men for me. Indefinitely probably—but definitely not this summer. I need to figure out the stuff I was doing wrong. Change. Change into being more of the person I want to be. Oh, God, it's so boring hearing someone talk about this kind of thing, isn't it? I'm sorry. I just wanted to be clear—"

"Amanda."

"Yes." He'd leaned forward, with such a serious expression, that she leaned forward, too.

"It's pretty obvious we've been worried about the same thing, don't you think? Both of us have these… life plans. About not getting involved with anyone right now. About needing to concentrate on nothing but parenting for a stretch. So we both agree…it'd be a real pain in the keester if you and I…" He motioned with his hands.

She nodded vigorously. "It would just be completely awkward."

He filled in more. "It'd be complicating. Unsettling. Exactly what neither of us want right now."

"I couldn't possibly agree more!"

He nodded. "So let's get this over with, okay? We'd better find out how dangerous the problem is before figuring out how to handle it."

Chapter Four

Granted, Amanda had had almost two glasses of wine—and before dinner, besides. So she realized she was a little addled, but she was still astonished when Mike—out of the complete blue—pulled her onto his lap.

The last she knew, they'd been talking, not flirting.

The last she knew—positively—they'd been talking about celibacy. His intention to be celibate. Her intention to be celibate. Their completely agreeing with each other.

So the fire started from nothing, came from nowhere. The smolder and snap of sparks suddenly caught, and just as suddenly spread. The heat startled her nerves, her skin, turned her senses incredibly tender. Smoke clogged her brain and fogged her vision. Sirens echoed in her ears—not sirens communicating danger, but a siren song calling mesmerizing, wicked things to her.

It was just a kiss, for Pete's sake.

She'd been kissing boys since she was fourteen. She'd been married. There wasn't a reason in the universe that this one should be so different.

But it was.

He was.

He'd kind of tumbled her onto his lap. His mouth had found hers before she'd found her balance. It was just all suddenly…there. The solid warmth of his body. The strength in his thighs and chest, the manly smell of him, the swoop of his arms creating a natural cradle.

And then there was the whole problem with his mouth. His lips were softer than butter. He offered a skim of a taste, then settled in, in a tangle of his taste and hers, the combination unexpectedly explosive.

She figured she should raise her hand and express a little outrage…but she couldn't seem to conjure any up. Objections appeared in the back of her mind, but never showed up at the front door.

This wasn't *nice*.

He didn't kiss *nice*.

He kissed as if he wanted to swallow her whole.

As if no touch, no kiss, no woman had ever ransomed his attention as she did.

Thrills shot through her blood as if she were on a roller-coaster ride.

She shifted, accidentally jamming her elbow into his ribs—but she had to look at him, had to catch her breath. His eyes were as glazed as hers. His breath coming as heavy. His frown just as dark.

But that made no sense. She went back for another kiss, to figure out what was really going on. A kiss—a few kisses—couldn't rock a girl's world. It had to be something else. Maybe some unusual kind of allergy attack. Or maybe pheromones were raining down from the sky. There had to be *something* that could be logically explained if she just studied it long enough.

So she studied a long, deep, eyes-closed kiss on him. The experiment failed. It seemed... Well, it seemed that she couldn't argue with a tsunami. She wrapped her arms around him, held on and just hoped she didn't drown—or if she was stuck drowning, that he was going down with her.

She felt his fingers tangling in her hair, holding her still, felt the sudden hard tumescence against her thigh, heard the shuddering breath coming out of him as he lifted his head...then dove back for more of that tsunami business.

A few hours later, she lifted her head.

Conceivably only a few minutes had passed, but

definitely long enough for her to feel both exhausted and energized. Exhausted, as if she craved a nap. Energized, as if the only thing she could think of was jumping him.

He had dark brown eyes. Liquid brown. The bad-boy disreputable attitude was gone. Now, she suspected that attitude thing was just a defense. This man, the Mike so close she could see every line and bone on his face, was as serious about life as she was.

Maybe even as vulnerable.

"I think," he said slowly, "that we just both found out how big the problem is." He helped her off his lap. They were both standing against each other for a millisecond, but Mike swiftly retreated to the side of the deck rail.

"A major uh-oh," she echoed, trying to make her voice sound light and easy. She didn't want him realizing how wild she'd felt in his arms. How crazy. How totally unlike herself.

"I wasn't trying to start trouble, I swear."

"I wasn't, either."

"But I did think…there was chemistry. That we'd both likely feel easier with each other once we figured out what was what. We'd already tried being honest with each other—about where we were in our lives."

"I'm always happier with honesty. No pretending. Not for me. No faking, no denying, none of that nonsense." She meant it. She'd lived the Prince Charming/princess fantasy her entire life. She was through with it.

He caught his breath. Or most of it. "Amanda. I'd appreciate a friend. I mean it. It'd be good for Ted to be around another woman besides his mother. I'd appreciate hearing how you think he's doing, from another single parent's perspective."

"And I'd appreciate a friend just as much. You've already proven to be a friend, Mike. And it sounds as if we're both going through a lot of the same problems. Grandparent issues. Ex issues. The same culture shock of moving to the suburbs. There are things we could laugh about. Talk through."

"As long as we don't let sex get in the way." Again, those fierce brown eyes met hers.

Again, she saw a different man than the rascal she'd first met. The sharp lines on his brow hadn't come from a devil-may-care type of guy. "Then we won't," she said firmly.

"We're agreed?"

"Completely, totally agreed," she said. "You know the lasagna I promised you?"

"Yup."

She motioned to the rough wood table on his deck. "Let's try it tomorrow. All of us. Give me a chance to spend a little time with your Teddy. For you to see my daughter. Let's see if they can be friends together, as well."

"Good idea," he said.

She thought so, too. Until she woke that night in the darkness, her whole body turned on by a wildly romantic dream. He was her prince. She was his princess. They were in a wild, erotic, exotic lovemaking fest, chasing each other through the sky, mating in sunlight, then moonlight, then snuggling together on a tuft of clouds.

Oh, no, she thought, too exasperated to sleep now. She got up, got a glass of water, checked on Molly, prowled the perimeter of the house. That kind of dream was not for her. Ever again.

"Okay. Now here's the deal." It was all Mike could do to subdue his excited son. Teddy had already run outside naked this morning, completely forgetting his clothes. He'd been conned into dressing—at least putting on a pj top and shorts—before galloping back out again.

They were digging the water garden—alias frog pond—today. The parts that appealed to Teddy, in order, were mud, shovels, water and frogs.

Mike had set up the design as simple as he could. "So...this is how we're going to do it. We're both going to dig inside this triangle area. *Nowhere* else. The dirt we're going to put in those wheelbarrows." He pointed to the two wheelbarrows. "*Nowhere* else."

"Got it, Dad. Can I dig now?"

"In a minute. When the hole's deep enough, I'm going to put in a liner. You can help me. And then we're going to set out rocks as a border, kind of make a triangle-shaped place to sit, where we can watch the frogs."

"Ok. Can I dig now?"

"There'll be a motor. To keep the water aerated and clean."

"Yeah. Can I—?"

"Yes." Mike gave up and let him loose.

He heard voices from next door, figured out immediately that Amanda and her daughter had yard work on their Saturday-morning agenda, too.

Their setup was slightly different from his.

For one thing, Molly wore a pink tutu, and had a pink crown on her head, and she did a lot of twirling. On his side of the driveway, Teddy was covered in mud and water inside of three minutes, and had managed to throw dirt everywhere but in the wheelbarrow.

The same sing-song refrain echoed from both yards, all variations of "Look at me, Dad!" or "Look at me, Mommy!"

Her yard had a pitcher with ice cubes and lemonade and cups and napkins.

He used a hose, both to get himself and Teddy clean enough to drink, and then to drink from.

A good hour passed, maybe two. The sun poured down, a hot liquid light. The pond got dug. All it cost were four Band-Aids, heaps of sunscreen, two or three pulled muscles in Mike's back, several buckets of sweat and a few torn clothes. The water garden was going to be darned nice when it was done, but Mike already knew it'd take eons more hours—after Teddy was in bed.

He stood up, gauging how much more he could get done before lunch, when he suddenly heard...silence. He glanced up, and saw the two redheads standing at the border of their yard. The one in the tutu had her hands on her hips and was staring at him with both disgust and fascination. Molly's mom looked as delectably dangerous as she had last night—only, last night she'd come undone in his arms. Today, she was wearing white shorts to garden, which he couldn't believe. And the pretty little bed of day lilies she'd planted looked ready for a garden show.

"We like your water garden," she called over.

"Your mommy is never going to let you in the house," Molly informed Mike, which seemed a fair indication he was wearing half the dirt in the yard.

"Molly—" Amanda started to address her daughter, but suddenly the miniature redhead shrieked.

"Mommy! Teddy's going pee pee outside! I can see it!"

Aw, well. Teddy undoubtedly hadn't wanted to waste time going all the way in the house to the bathroom when they were having so much fun. It likely never occurred to him that squirting on the back fence might not be the best idea. Mike rubbed a hand over his face, trying to figure out what to say or do, accidentally got a piece of dirt in his eye.

Then the barking started. Slugger had been outside with them, but pretty much he'd just been basking in the sunlight and snoozing—that was, until the Sissy Dog somehow escaped a tether on their back porch and came prancing over, a diamond-studded leash trailing behind her.

Slugger could move fast. It just wasn't usually his choice.

The girls took off after "Darling." Mike took off after Slugger. How her dog knew about dog doors, he had no idea, but the little squirt shot into his house, followed immediately by his lovesick hound. Molly tried to crawl through the dog door. Then Teddy showed up and the kids tangled in the doorway.

Normally Mike would have let Amanda through before him, but just then he figured that chivalry was less important than preventing the dogs from having an inappropriate hookup. He might have wished he'd had a fresh shower. That his house looked a little less like a tornado site. That the path wasn't littered with shoes and toys. Cat screeched from the top of the mantel at the hullabaloo.

The kids were circling, calling for the dogs—at least, until her Molly got sidetracked by a toy. Naturally Teddy stopped to explain the toy to her, and that left only the two adults searching high and low for the dogs—who'd suddenly turned quiet.

"Not a good sign," Mike admitted to her.

The canines weren't in the laundry room—which had wash heaped to the ceiling. Clean wash, not dirty wash. All the same, Mike so far hadn't thought of a reason why it had to be folded or put away when they could both just take stuff off the pile when they needed clean clothes. Amanda shot him a look.

"What? What?"

"Someday your son's going to get married. Which means you'll have a daughter-in-law. And she'll blame you if your son expects her to pick up after him."

"Huh?"

He pushed into his bedroom first—worried what she'd see—but it was fairly picked up. Just an unmade king-size bed, the sunlight hitting on the steel-gray sheets and striped blanket. "No dogs," he said when he spotted a jockstrap on the master-bathroom floor, and closed the door as he ushered her out.

There was no sign of the dogs in Teddy's room, either, but she got a good look. "You decorated to beat the band in here," she noted.

"I wouldn't call it decorating."

"I'm just saying—you went to a lot of trouble. And it shows. What a great room for a boy."

Maybe so, but that wasn't solving their dog-disappearance problem. Mike shut the bedroom door to close off another potential egress—or exit—depending on which the dogs tried for next. "There's nothing upstairs but a big loft—it's the play-room," he told her, and then stopped talking, because he heard sounds. Odd sounds. Very odd, yowly, ca-nine sounds.

"Stay here," he told the kids, which had all the effect of a whisper on a flood. He took the steps two at a time, but the kids still beat him to the top.

Molly, who could outrun a quarterback, even in her tutu, let out a scream that could have shattered glass. "Mommy! Slugger's hurting Darling! He's being mean! Make him stop it!"

"He *isn't* being mean," Teddy told her, and tugged hard on Mike's arm. "Dad, I don't get it. What's Slug-ger doing?"

The loft was divided into father and son spaces. On Mike's side, there was a computer and desk, battered couch, pool table, wall-mounted TV. On Teddy's side, there was a town of trucks, a train set, a washing-machine box with doors and windows cut out, shelves with games and books.

Slugger and Darling were pretty much on the line between spaces, getting it on with abandon. Well, maybe not abandon. Darling looked fairly bored. Slugger looked more animated than Mike had ever seen him.

Amanda looked at them—then him—with hor-ror.

"You didn't tell me she was in heat," Mike said.

"I didn't think she was. There was no sign. And I thought she was too young!"

"Um. It'd appear she's definitely old enough." Mike struggled to find a positive. "At least she wasn't a thoroughbred."

"That's not the point! She was mixed to be mixed with her own kind! Because it's such a good—"

"Mix. Yeah, I got it." Mike scraped a hand through his hair. "Kids, go downstairs."

"Mommy, make him stop jumping on Darling!"

"Can't you do something?" Amanda demanded.

"At this point, they look pretty well…hooked up. I'm not sure how to de-hook them. If it'd hurt them."

"I just can't believe this," Amanda said with despair.

"Neither can I." Mike sighed. "I'm guessing this means that I won't get that lasagna tonight, huh?"

Princess, Darling, Molly and Amanda were all crowded into the downstairs bathroom. Someone had originally painted the room green. As soon as Amanda could get the supplies purchased—there was so much to do in a new house—the girls had decided it was turning into their butterfly room. The grape-and-aqua butterfly wallpaper had already been decided on. But that subject had already been thoroughly discussed, and they were on to the next.

Dinner next door.

Because Molly no longer wanted to go, Amanda was determined to turn the occasion into a solid parenting lesson...but so far, that was challenging.

"I don't see why we have to eat with them, Mom."

Molly, in spite of her current scowl, looked downright adorable in her purple-and-white shorts set. Because she claimed she was way too old for a nap these days, she'd been coaxed into supervising a rest period for Darling and Princess. All three had conked out for a good hour's snooze.

Amanda wrapped a purple scrunchie in Molly's hair, making a tidy ponytail that matched her own. She was also wearing a purple-and-white shorts set. Personally, she was a little freaked to do the matching mom-daughter clothing thing, but Molly had claimed it was the "most important thing to her in the whole world."

"We're going over there for dinner," Amanda explained, "because we want to show Mr. Mike and Teddy that we're gracious."

"What's *gracious?*" Molly studied her mom as Amanda put on mascara.

"Being gracious means... Well, things weren't going too well between us all this morning, right?"

"You're not kidding. I couldn't believe Teddy peed in the yard. I didn't see his penis, but I still saw him peeing. And then his dog hurt our dog. And then they were so *dirty.*"

"Well, honey, Darling wasn't really hurt by their Slugger. That was something else. But the point—about our going, about our being gracious—is that strong girls don't run away where there's a problem."

"Why not?"

"Because the problem's still waiting for you when you stop running. So it's just a whole lot easier if you just deal with a problem right when it happens."

"But I don't have a problem. *They* have a problem. Can I put on that stuff on my eyes, like you?"

"Not mascara, lovebug. But we'll do blush together." Molly immediately lifted her face and closed her eyes, waiting for her mom to brush her cheeks. Immediately she peered at herself in the mirror.

"I look beautiful," she said with awe.

"Yes, you do. You look beautiful, but even more important, you're going to be gracious, and polite and on your best manners."

"Why do I have to be on my best manners again?" Molly insisted.

"Because they're neighbors. And we want them to be good neighbors. So we're going to show them that we're nice people. Everybody has problems come up, honey. Friends, neighbors, family. Disagreements don't disappear if you ignore them." She'd been an expert at doing just that, all her life, and particularly in her marriage. So for damn sure, Molly wasn't going to make the same mistakes. "We're going to be on our very, very, very best behavior, okay?"

"Got it. We'll show 'em. I'm going to be so good you won't believe it. I'm going to be so good you'll probably want to get me an outfit for my American Girl doll. I'm going to be so good that you'll let me stay u—"

"We're both going to be on our best manners because it's a good idea. But we'll talk about that other stuff when we get home." Amanda didn't want to commit to bribery. Unless she had to. In the meantime, there was still a ton to get ready before heading next door. Darling had to be walked—on a leash. Princess expected a treat right before dinner. Amanda had to unearth the picnic basket, then start stacking the dinner—the hot plate of lasagna, silverware, napkins, a warm towel-wrapped loaf of Italian bread, a chilled bowl of fruits for salad. There was also carrot cake with a butterscotch sauce, but she couldn't carry it all at once. Truthfully, she couldn't carry what she had now.

"I'll help, Mommy." Using her most virtuous voice, Molly reached for the napkins.

"Thanks, honey." Amanda tried to keep the irony from her tone, took a breath, and off they went.

"Good grief," Mike said when he opened the back door. "Amanda, I figured you'd bring a pan, not a whole feast. You didn't have to go to all this trouble—"

Oh, yeah, she did. Looking at that sweaty, oiled man all morning—shirtless, muscles gleaming, laughing with his son—well, the whole morning had put bad ideas in her mind, that was all. Unacceptable ideas. The trauma with the dogs was just a different layer of tension. She was living next door to this guy. She had to make it all more comfortable—a *lot* more comfortable—than she was feeling right now. And food seemed the best way to do it, because he was a guy.

Food always worked with guys.

"It was no trouble," her daughter informed him, in her best grown-up voice.

Mike, to give him credit, didn't laugh. "Well, we sure appreciate it," Mike told Molly with due seriousness, and then herded them all onto the shady back deck.

Not that Amanda wanted to dwell on it, but Mike definitely cleaned up well. A white polo set off his ruddy skin; the denim shorts even had a belt.

His hand touched her lower back for only a second, yet it was enough to put a tick in her pulse.

Teddy had been spruced up, too, his unruly hair still damp and hard-combed. The dog was completely out of sight, although there was a hint of mournful baying coming from the second floor. The deck table had been cleaned off. The view overlooked their almost-finished water garden.

The kids sat across from each other, while Mike

and Amanda unpacked the picnic basket. "That's an amazing project you took on," she said, wanting her voice to come out as cheerful as a stranger's. Specifically, she wanted to sound like an unfamiliar woman he'd never kissed, and for damn sure, never rattled.

"It's going to take a lot of hours of blood, sweat and tears, but I'm hoping it'll turn out."

His son piped up, "We're gonna put frogs in the pond. And then we'll feed them our own worms."

"Yuck! Mommy," Molly said.

"Remember. Gracious." At Amanda's reminder, Molly bobbed her head in exuberant agreement. And that was when the whole dinner started a crash-dive that just never recovered.

Her sweet daughter looked up at Mike. "We're going to be gracious to you two even if you're complete pigs."

Amanda winced.

"Well. We'll try not to be pigs for you," Mike told her. "What would you kids like to drink?"

"Root beer," his son answered, where Molly said, "Iced tea with a little sugar and a little lemon and two small ice cubes. But not too big a glass because I could spill it. And I can't spill it because I'm being extra polite today. Thank you. Oh. I mean, please. Right, Mommy?"

Amanda glanced under the table. Nope, no room to hide there.

Teddy said to his dad, "What's wrong with her?"

"Nothing's wrong with anyone," Mike said firmly, and stopped choking long enough to deliver drinks. Everyone but her suddenly impossibly fussy daughter were easily pleased by having only to pop a top.

For a short stretch, food captured everyone's attention. Molly sat next to her, crossing her legs exactly as Amanda did. Teddy looked at them both across the table as if they were as fascinating—almost—as dead animals. He started a steady round of kicking, only once in a while kicking Amanda—which was far, far better, she thought, than the Armageddon that would follow if he accidentally kicked Molly.

But those few moments of good luck just couldn't hold. She'd never seen anyone eat as much as Mike— easy proof he was nuts for lasagna. Both kids gained red stains on their clothes, but that was to be expected. One drink spilled. A nearby bee made Molly shriek. Their golden cat with the scary eyes attempted several times to leap on the table.

But it was almost over—and nothing too terrible had happened—until the subject of sex came up.

It wasn't exactly Mike's fault. Everybody was shoveling in food, and Mike took the occasion of quiet to murmur sotto voce, "So…did you have the chance to call your vet?"

She answered carefully. "Yes. At least, I reached her office. She's not in for the next few days. The receptionist said there's a type of morning-after pill. I'm not sure if it applies. We'll see."

"I told you I'd pay."

"Not necessary," Amanda started to say, but hearing the words *we'll see* triggered a knee-jerk response in her daughter.

"Yeah. You know what *we'll see* means. It means we'll talk about it later. That's what Mom said about what your dog was doing to our dog."

"Now, Molly, I didn't—"

Molly had hunched forward, was looking both male Conroys in the eye with her drama-queen face on. "I don't get it. Why your dog would hurt my Darling. My dog is sweet and wonderful. I can't believe you'd let your dog be so mean."

"Honey," Amanda said again, but she was drowned out by Teddy's voice.

"*My* dog isn't mean. *My* dog is the best dog in the whole world. Your dog must have done something," Teddy informed her.

"*My* dog didn't do *anything*. That's why I named her Darling. Because she's a darling. And your dog was *hurting* her."

"He was not!"

"Kids," Amanda said, "Neither dog was hurting the other. Molly, we talked about this."

"No, we didn't. You just said the dogs were playing. They weren't playing. I don't know why you're not telling me the truth, but I know what the truth is this time," Molly said, and turned again to Teddy. "I *saw* it. I *saw* your dog on top of my dog. I think your dog should say he's sorry!"

"Hold it, both of you," Mike said firmly. "Neither dog was being mean. Neither dog was hurting the other. What was going on was…"

He glanced at Amanda, as if asking permission. But as much as she wanted to make the situation better, right then, she was busy wiping up lasagna spots from the table.

So Mike said, "Listen up. That's just what a boy and girl dog do when they really, really like each other."

"Why?" Teddy asked.

"Yeah, why?" Molly echoed.

Again Mike looked at Amanda, this time more desperately. She reached for a spoonful of fruit salad. "Okay," he said, "but you owe me for this." And to the kids, he continued, "Because that's how dogs express when they love each other and want to have puppies."

"But I love puppies," Molly said.

"Everybody loves puppies."

"But you and Mommy were all upset. Why were you all upset if we were going to get puppies!"

"Because," he said, and almost for sure Amanda felt a big bare hairy foot tapping her ankle, "your dog is very young. And we adults felt that maybe she was too young to have puppies quite yet. That it wouldn't be good for her until she was a little older."

"I know what you're talking about now," Teddy piped in. "It's sex. I know all about it," he informed Molly. "I've got a book and everything. I can't read yet, but it's got pictures of frog babies and duck babies and stuff. I'm probably going to learn to read next year."

"I don't care about sex and reading! I care about puppies!" Molly said.

"That's just because you're a girl and you're stupid."

"Stop right there!" Both parents said simultaneously. The potential for war simmered in the air, the kids glaring at each other nonstop...but then Teddy said he had to go to the bathroom.

"You're not going to pee in the yard again, are you?" Molly asked with horror.

Teddy looked at his dad. "You told me I had to be nice. I *been* nice. I been *totally* nice. But I can't be nice *all* the time."

"Just go to the bathroom and we'll talk about it later."

When Teddy headed into the house, Amanda jumped up and started heaping dishes back in the picnic basket. Her daughter was trying to engage Mike in a further discussion of sex and puppies— Molly had a backbone of steel, and when she wanted something, such as puppies, she could be relentless.

There'd be another chance. Hopefully. Maybe. Conceivably. But right now, keeping the kids together any longer was like rubbing poison ivy on bare skin. The gathering tonight needed a fast curtailment. Amanda figured that the faster they got out of there, the better.

"So," Molly continued to grill Mike, "how come people have babies? How come people can't have puppies instead?"

A crash from just inside the house startled the three of them. Mike shot out of his seat, and Amanda was right behind him. Crashes and four-year-olds were never a good sign.

Chapter Five

Amanda only had to step into Mike's living room to grasp the big picture. Near the fireplace, a table lamp had fallen to the ground, its shade askew, its lightbulb and ceramic base in pieces. A tennis ball was in sight. And Teddy was standing in the bathroom doorway. The instant he heard his dad bang through the screen door, he started crying.

"It wasn't me, Dad! I didn't do it! It wasn't me!"

Amanda watched Mike charge over to his son—initially, she was unsure whether he was angry or annoyed or frustrated. But his response conveyed none of those things. He just swiftly scooped up his son and lifted him away from the sharp shards.

Teddy heaved sobs in between extensive explanations to his dad.

"It was a woman who did it. She came in the front door. I said who are you and you'd better get out of here. But she picked up Slugger's ball and threw it at the lamp just like that. I couldn't stop her. I wasn't strong enough. I said, I'm going to get my dad! But then she ran away! It wasn't me, Dad! It was her! The woman!"

Mike set his son on a chair—firmly—with a glance at Amanda.

"Where's your broom or vacuum?" she asked.

"I'll take care of it."

"I'm telling you the *truth,* Dad. She had yellow hair. And she was tall. And she had a big purse. And big, big, big earrings."

"Teddy," Mike said quietly, sternly. "Your mother was not here."

"It wasn't my mother. It was just a woman who looked like her. And had earrings like her. I told her and told her, go away and I'll call my dad. But she still just picked up Slugger's ball…"

Amanda figured it was an ideal time to tiptoe away. She grabbed Molly and the picnic basket and took off for home.

It was another four hours before she could call the day quits. All through the kitchen cleanup and story reads and putting Molly to bed, she kept thinking about Mike—about how he was with his son.

They both had their share of parenting challenges. But she liked how he'd handled Teddy with gentle, calm firmness. How his first thought was to rescue his son from potential harm, not to scold. And how Teddy showed no fear of his dad, only absolute, secure trust, even when the squirt had been inventing an incredibly wild story and had to know there'd be some punishment for throwing the ball in the house and breaking the lamp.

She folded the dish towel, poured a glass of sun tea, turned off lights and ambled outside. Instead of choosing a chair or the chaise, she perched on the deck steps.

The sun had just dropped out of sight, but there was still ample light to see the backyard and the plantings she'd done that morning. Robins pranced in the grass. A dove cooed from the shadows.

Slowly, the sky deepened, softened, darkened. She sipped her tea, set it down, stretched out her legs, relaxed. Stars popped into the sky, which was hardly a surprise on a cloudless night...but suddenly there seemed to be stars in the grass, as well. She sat up, confused, figuring the twinkling lights on the ground had to be some kind of optical illusion. The tiny lights switched on, off, one after the other, all through the yard. Five, then a dozen, then more.

It was crazy. She wandered into the yard, feeling the tickly brush of soft grass beneath her bare feet, and extended a hand…something touched her, then lit up. Another one of those impossible "stars."

"Fireflies. Amazing, aren't they?"

She whirled around, saw Mike's shadow from his deck, and immediately felt her pulse kick up. It was because she wanted to talk to him, of course. It wasn't chemistry. It was that debacle at dinner that she wanted to discuss.

He aimed down the steps, into her yard. Her heartbeat did more of that frisky thing…but there were stars floating and dancing around them, on an evening turned velvet dark, and the man looked downright magical, coming out of the shadows like a prince in a fairy tale.

Obviously her mind couldn't be trusted.

"I've never seen them before. Fireflies? So they're an insect?"

"And ugly in daylight. But they don't bite or sting or hurt anything. They're just putting out flashes to attract the opposite sex."

Like him, she thought. The damned man kept putting out flashes, forcing her pulse to do that thrum thing, making her somehow want to lean closer to him. Not that she did any such thing. "You recovered from dinner? And just for the record, I think you're a hero for taking on the sex-education questions."

He gave a short laugh. "Your daughter had me stumped with the question about why humans have babies and can't have puppies. Not that it's a hard question. Just hard to think up an answer that works for a four-year-old."

"Speaking of four-year-olds…I swear, Mike, my daughter can be absolutely wonderful."

He chuckled again. "I think she is. She's honest. And she stands up. My guess is that all that character comes from the red hair. Your set of genes." And then it was his turn to clear his throat. "And speaking of the other four-year-old…I swear, my son does know how to tell the truth."

"Of course he does. That's just what four-year-olds do. Invent. Imagine. It just gets out of control sometimes."

Mike scraped a hand through his hair. "Well, in my time, we called it lying. The tricky part is that the villain in all his stories is never an ogre or an alligator or a bad guy. It's always a woman who looks just like his mom."

Amanda winced—for both of them. "Touchy." She didn't motion him toward the steps, but they both seem to aim back there. He took one side and she took the other, neither touching…neither even looking at each other. She thought they were both being seriously smart this time.

Besides, there were those magical fireflies to look at.

"You weren't kidding about Teddy having mom issues, were you? Or mom-desertion issues."

He sighed. "I keep trying to turn it around, but I'm

not sure how. I was a lawyer by profession, did I tell you that? Right and wrong questions are supposed to be easy. But even when a divorce is right…even when both sides do their best…it's never so easy for the kids."

"Totally agree." She tried not to turn her head. "You're not working now?"

"No. When I left the downtown firm I was employed by, it wasn't just the divorce, but wanting something with less pressure, less hours, for Teddy's sake. I really wanted to take a couple months off, go after a healthier life here. A kid's life, rather than an adult's city life. All the stuff we talked about before. Speaking of which…do you know what you're doing for preschools?"

She started to laugh…and then he did, too.

"I know," he said wryly. "I can remember when I had the spare time for music, restaurants, a show, whatever. Now it's analyzing what makes a four-year-old fib and deciding whether he needs vaccination shots for preschool. What happened to my real life and will it ever show up again?"

Amanda felt a heart tug…she could have asked the exact same question, and she couldn't believe there was someone else who understood exactly what she was going through. This kind of talk…it wasn't like leaning. It wasn't like counting on a white knight to rescue her. It was just…incredible…to find someone else who needed to reach out for the same reasons.

A friend.

A plain old real friend.

What a wild concept.

"What?" he said, as if trying to read her expression.

"Nothing. I just… It's nice to laugh. Just laugh. Just be with someone else," she said honestly.

"Yeah. No strings. No weirdness. No worrisome anything."

"Exactly," she said, and in that peaceful moment, her sanity took a complete nosedive. There was no explaining it. Mike lurched up from the deck steps to stand up, and start for home. She stood up at the same time, thinking it was time to turn in. Screen doors were open; it's not as if they couldn't hear their kids, but it had been a long day. She suspected he was as ready for an early night as she was, and started to say so.

Only, their shoulders accidentally grazed again, when they were both in motion. And because it was dark, she stumbled on the bottom step. He caught her, kept her from falling. They were still laughing…but then she lifted her laughing face up to his, intending to say something warm and friendly.

Suddenly there was a second of silence. As magical as the firefly night. As compelling as water and food and shelter. As restlessly disturbing as the air just before a thunderstorm.

And then the storm hit.

These weren't like the kisses before. This was Gorilla Glue. Once he pulled her into his arms, she couldn't pull free. Once her mouth found his, he either couldn't or wouldn't let go.

He spun her—possibly just an instinctive moment to protect them both from falling. Whatever the reason, he whirled her down the step, into the grass, into the dark shadows of the yard. A simple turn somehow escalated into a wild, crazy dance. A dance of kisses. A dance of stolen laughter. A dance of silliness at first, yet transformed by the rhythm of silk and shadows into something darker, richer. Sexier.

He murmured something, into her hair, onto her throat, a whisper that tickled her skin, tingled her senses. She lifted her arms to loop around his neck, wanting to look at him, to understand what was going on.

He looked back, but his eyes were too dark, too mesmerizing. His palms skidded down her sides, taking in ribs, waist, hips, shaping her, learning her. Then he bent down for another sweep of a kiss, this one involving teeth and tongues and pressure.

She curved closer, spine bowed, so her breasts and belly could rub against him. She hadn't felt this ignition charge since...since he'd first kissed her. But that was controllable. This wasn't. The divorce had brought on an epic stretch of sexual deprivation. But desire so fierce, so luscious, that she couldn't catch her breath?

He made her feel it. The desire to risk all. The brand of need that tangled every nerve in the body. Abandonment. That's what she wanted. Just once in her life. To abandon all reason, all good sense, and just give into the power of this man, this moment, this incredibly powerful wildness.

A dog suddenly barked. Not his hound. Not her Darling. A neighbor's dog…reminding her—and apparently Mike—that they were in the middle of a neighborhood. His head shot up. She lifted hers at the same time.

This wasn't a Shangri-la with fireflies.

It wasn't a fantasy.

It was real life. With both their kids behind screened doors mere yards away.

"Good grief," she murmured, aware that her shorts seemed to be unbuttoned, her tee dragging off her shoulder. That his tee had been pushed up. Possibly even by her…since no one else appeared to be glued to him.

"Hell," he responded. Then, "You want to hear I'm sorry?"

"No, of course not. It just…happened. I don't believe you planned this. And I sure as heavens didn't."

He nodded, relief in his face as he stepped back.

"Good thing we understand each other. Nice to have a friend where you don't have to sweat guilt or regrets or explanations all the time."

"You said it," she said. Somehow her voice came out oddly hollow. "Thank heavens we're just friends."

Thankfully, sanity returned with daylight…and more sanity shored up after days passed without seeing her neighbor. The mosquito bites faded. The mark on her throat slowly disappeared. The raw feeling in her heart… Well, she banished it. As she was sure Mike had.

They'd been a pinch away from making love. Outside. In the grass. With the fireflies and mosquitoes. In public.

Well.

That certainly wouldn't happen again.

"When's Daddy coming?" Molly asked—for the fifth time in the past five minutes.

Thom had been due a half hour ago. "Any minute now."

"He said we were going to do something special. He said it was a surprise."

"I know, sweetheart."

"Daddy said he's going to buy me a bunch of stuff."

"Did he?" Amanda lifted the brush. They'd already done Molly's hair. Twice. But Molly wanted it "perfect."

"Daddy said we'll have so much fun that I can stay overnight next time."

"I'm sure he believes that's true, lovebug." And it would happen when hell froze over, but Amanda didn't say that to Miss Priss. The outfit for the day, after long deliberation, was a panda-bear tee in purple and pink, pink capris, sandals with panda-shaped bows and, of course, sunglasses with the same motif. Molly, naturally, had coordinated it all.

Amanda contributed a bag with bug spray, sunscreen and a variety of healthy snacks to hand to her ex. The jerk wouldn't think of any of that. He'd be too busy buying off his daughter.

Just a half hour before, the mail had arrived— and she'd gotten the letter from Friend of the Court, expressing Thom's request for full joint custody. She knew why he wanted it. So he could cut her child support.

"Can I go outside, Mom?"

"Sure. We'll wait outside."

Thom was just pulling in. The car was brand-new, a gleaming black hybrid. The devil stepped out, looking handsome as sin—white smile, cool shades, the same elegant posture and walk that had drawn her attention to begin with.

It was embarrassing to remember how naive she'd been back then.

Molly yelled, "Daddy!" And he swung her up and around in his arms as if hoping the whole world was watching—with a camera—so he could prove how much his daughter adored him.

Which Molly certainly did. She chattered ten for a dozen as she crawled into the backseat, automatically strapping herself into the child's seat. He glanced up, said, "Amanda" as if he'd just noticed her.

"You'll have her back by seven?" Amanda said.

"I'm sure you'll call me if I'm five minutes late."

His tone was snotty. She let it go.

Still, seeing him invariably provoked some icky memories. Discovering all Thom's cheating had been a blow—but the worse blow had been his explanations. He actually believed that he was entitled. That casual sex with others "didn't take anything away" from her. He believed they had a terrific life, including a great sex life, so what he did in his spare time would never have mattered, if she just hadn't found out.

Oh, yeah. He'd also mentioned that becoming a mother had made her less physically attractive, less attentive, less adventurous and fun.

He must have thought she needed that extra kick in the teeth.

Now she thought…maybe she had. Because that fight had given her the momentum to kick him out.

She waved goodbye to Molly until the black car turned the corner, then whipped around. She had tons to do today. Drapes. Closet organizing. Rug issues. All the kinds of new-home projects that were boring for Molly, and Amanda could accomplish twice as fast if she were alone.

She'd just reached for the front doorknob when a car pulled into Mike's driveway. Two people emerged from the steel-gray Volvo. The woman, stepping from the passenger side, was a stunner. Salon blond. Tall and sleek, doing the safari linen and khaki style thing. A toned figure that made any normal woman want to slap her.

Mike's ex, Amanda assumed.

But the car's driver was the shocker. The man climbing from the driver's seat was sneezing into a handkerchief. He was a little guy with a sweet face and a comb-over. He wore an immaculate white polo, with creased shorts that unfortunately revealed bony, ropy legs. Possibly he weighed in at one hundred and fifty pounds, after a stuffed dinner. Possibly.

She wasn't *staring*. She'd have gone right back in her house, except that Mike's front door opened, and out zoomed the hound, the cat, Teddy and finally Mike.

The hound and cat looked excited to see the visitors. Teddy was hanging on tightly to Mike's hand.

The driver of the car took one look at the animals, and dove back in the car, sneezing several times in succession. Mike, who had a disreputable look to start with, looked even less shaved, less brushed, less kempt than usual. More sexy. But he definitely had made a point of looking just-woken-up and didn't-give-a-royal-fig.

The blonde crossed the walk, bent down, took Teddy's hand. The squirt was holding back tears, but he talked to his mother and was eventually coaxed into the backseat of the Volvo.

"I'll have a cell phone on all day," Mike told her.

"He'll be fine with me." To Teddy, in a sugary voice, she said, "We're going to have a great day, honey, I promise. And George is really looking forward to our day together."

When the Volvo backed out of the driveway, Mike was still standing there, flanked by the hound and the cat. He spotted her when he turned.

Amanda had a flashback of fireflies and a wild, erotic mating dance...but she tamped that memory down. "*What* was that?" she asked.

"You mean, the guy?"

"Yeah."

"He's one of the main reasons I gave up sex after the divorce."

She'd done a fine job of steering clear of him for almost a week, but shoot. There were some things she could resist. This wasn't one of them. "I'm bringing fresh coffee," she said, went into her house, refilled her mug, filled one for him and crossed the driveways to his front porch.

He was sitting on the front step, with his critters. Cat wasn't about to budge, but the hound made room for her.

He accepted the mug, took a long deep slug of it. Said, "George is a germ freak. He's afraid of dirt and germs. Or about everything important in a little boy's life. Teddy can't do anything right when he's over there—and I'm going to worry about him the whole damned day."

"I would, too."

"I don't want to talk about it," he said firmly, and then, "She's not pushing for custody. Good thing. Because I'd fight her to the wall. But I can't deny her time with Teddy. I mean, she's his mother, for God's sake."

"I understand."

"I don't want to talk about it," he said again, took another gulp of coffee, hunched elbows on his knees and then went on. "I couldn't believe it when I found out she was cheating. I know this sounds damned egotistical, but I honestly believed that part of our lives was fine. Better than fine. So the worst part was finding out she was cheating with *him*."

Since he'd already finished his mug, she handed him hers. She wasn't drinking more coffee anyway. She tried not to breathe. She didn't want anything diverting him from telling her more of the story.

He shot a gesture to the sky. Not the middle-finger gesture. Just a frustrated gesture. "If she was going to cheat, at least it could have been with a better-looking guy. A richer guy. Someone who had some appeal, I could see. But Mr. Dork there? Talk about a kick in the nuts. Not that I want to talk about it."

"I can see you don't."

"But then and there, I voted for celibacy for the rest of my life. I mean, I admit, I worked long hours. But I also made good money. When Teddy was born, I brought in help for her, with the baby and the house. Made sure she had private time to see her friends, take on projects, not always feel tied down. And she was a good mom. I thought. And I thought I was making time for the two of us. We still went out. Did things. Hell. I didn't even know she was unhappy. She just said out of the blue that she was leaving. For George. And told our son that we hadn't gotten along, but Teddy never *saw* us not getting along. So he keeps saying he knows it was because he was too much trouble."

"Yikes," she said gently.

"He's *not* too much trouble. But that bozo makes it all worse, because Teddy can't please him. He really, really tries, but sooner or later, a glass of milk is going to spill. Or he'll forget to flush. Or he'll pick up something he's not supposed to touch. Or he'll do something wrong, on George's terms. Nobody yells at him. He just hates it there. You know what he tells me?"

"What?"

"That going there makes him sick to his stomach. *That's* why I did the worm farm. And dug the water garden in back. I just wanted to let him do certain things—make messes, get dirty. If he spills some water, putting water in the dish for the dog and cat, it's like, so what? He's learning to take care of pets, to look out for them. He's four. How is he supposed to do anything perfect when he's four?"

"Mike?"

"*What?*"

"It kills me, too. When I have to give up my kid for the day. And I had a huge list of stuff on the day's plate, from curtains to wallpaper to organizing closets. I still have dishes in boxes. And—"

"Good grief. I could get tired, just imagining you trying to accomplish all that."

"I'm tired, just thinking about it. Which kind of sparked a new thought." She hesitated, certain a bad idea was about to surface, yet for that precise second she couldn't analyze why it was so bad. "How about if we spend a few grown-up hours together? Have lunch out. Someplace you'd never take four-year-olds. Then see a movie. Something—*anything*—that's not a cartoon or has Disney anywhere in the credits."

He looked at her. She looked back. He said, "I'll change shoes and get my wallet."

"I have to take the dog out."

"Speaking of which—"

"No, she hasn't been to the vet yet. The whole

thing got kind of complicated. I had an appointment, then their office called and said the vet had a family emergency. But she's seeing Darling in two days. The appointment's made. So that's not a problem on the table today."

"Okay, then. Five minutes. Back here. My car?"

"Fine by me."

Chapter Six

Six hours later, Mike left the Dan Ryan—the expressway where faint-of-heart drivers were tortured at rush hour, a uniquely Chicagoan sport—and turned into the curve toward the western suburbs. They still wouldn't be home for another twenty minutes.

He didn't want the day to end.

He glanced at his passenger. Amanda had never said a word about riding in the pickup, but she was obviously comfortable. Even strapped in, she'd managed to curl her legs under her, had slipped off a sandal.

"This has been the best day," she murmured.

"You're not kidding." He'd been both wary and willing of playing hooky with her. Wary, because she already inspired too many wrong ideas and hormones. And yet willing, because...well, because after his ex-wife drove off, he'd still felt the rug burns on his ego.

Nancy had never said the exact words, but her opinion of him was clear. Lawyer or not, great education or not, he was still hopelessly rough-edged. Too earthy. Too physical. Too sexual. Her choosing 'George' pretty obviously underlined everything she'd found wrong with him. Maybe he'd achieved stature in a notable law firm, but that didn't give him elegance or taste by her standards.

Amanda was distinctly a woman of elegance and taste. So chances were she'd discover those rotten qualities and back off...or his own rug burns would make him too wary to get further involved.

All of which was to say...he'd been able to relax with her today.

Maybe even more than relax. They'd had just plain old ordinary fun. She'd picked the lunch spot, a place where she got to choose lobster bisque and he could vote for a raw red steak. Their entrees echoed how different they were, but that didn't seem to matter. The restaurant was packed with a professional lunch crowd. All adults. No spills, no screams, no, "I don't want this!" or "Are we done yet?" or "I'm bored, Dad!"

The movie was even better. She'd picked the restaurant, so he'd picked the movie. It was the first flick he'd seen in ages that had some skin, some blood, some action. She could eat the chocolate she wanted. He could have his own popcorn. No one whispered in his ear. No one claimed they had to go to the bathroom three times. He actually got to see a movie from start to end.

It's not as if this were a date....

He wasn't aware he'd spoken aloud, until Amanda chuckled. "Of course it wasn't a date. We're not *dating*. We just had a grown-up afternoon." She sighed with contentment. "No Bambi. No comic-book characters. And I had the whole chocolate bar."

He laughed. "You had two, I believe."

"Yeah, I admit I went overboard—but I haven't had a whole chocolate bar to myself in...well, in years. I'm always trying to think about setting the right example." She smiled at him again. "That's the best part. A whole afternoon without any 'shoulds' or 'have tos'."

Damned, if he didn't feel exactly the same way. It was funny, but he hadn't been easy in his own skin for a long time now. Certainly not when he was married. There always seemed to be something he was doing or saying wrong, something that was going to get analyzed and criticized.

It seemed unbelievable—if not downright crazy— that he could feel that rare sense of easiness with her.

By the time he pulled in his driveway, she was still

smiling...and so was he. "We have a couple of hours before the kids are due home," she said.

"Yeah. Both of us might even catch a nap or some reading time." He climbed out at the same time she did, stretched. Cat and Slugger burst out of the pet door as if they hadn't seen him in a decade. Cat slapped Slugger with a paw when the hound tried to reach him first. Slugger immediately howled, but he couldn't have been hurt too badly, because he kept galloping, ears flapping in the wind.

Amanda laughed and then kept on laughing. "I'm afraid I'll be greeted the same way when I walk in the door."

And she turned that way...but she didn't seem in any rush to race home. They both seemed to linger. Just standing there. He'd tried not to pay attention, but the warmth of late-afternoon sunshine brushed her shoulders, turned her hair into fire, and her eyes—he swore—were as emerald-green as the jewel.

"Well...thanks for a great afternoon," she said, and bounced up—as if she intended to give him a friendly, neighborly hug.

He thought that fast hug was a great idea—a way to underline how easily they were going to maintain the friendship thing. Only...once she lifted up on tiptoes, she seemed to hesitate. The shine in her eyes seemed to darken. He felt the brush of those sassy high breasts, the graze of her pelvis, the scent of her skin take over his air space.

In that spare second, he couldn't seem to breathe—except for her. Couldn't seem to move—because those basic touches ignited a maelstrom of furious wants and noisy needs. Couldn't seem to control the hunger—to kiss her again.

He didn't.

She didn't.

For a good, long three seconds.

It was her fault things changed, he was pretty sure, because she was the one who swung her arms around his neck. But then…hell. He couldn't keep his mouth off hers, and the kiss became a banquet of tasting, taking, wooing. He had to touch her. Had to. He stroked down her spine, the route not familiar, just familiar enough so that he knew the curve in her back, knew a palm on her fanny brought a groan… and encouraged her to lean even tighter into him.

Invitations hung in the air, unseen, invisible, but real as the sunlight. *Maybe* suddenly seemed the longest word in the English language, analyzed between her lips and his, between the silken brush of her hair in the breeze, between the heat he could feel rising in her skin, through her skin…into him.

She lifted her head, opened stunned-soft eyes, looked straight at him.

She swallowed. He got his breath back. She remembered to drop her hands from around his neck. He remembered to drop his hands from around her back. The flush on her cheeks—there was no changing that.

There was no changing the brick inside his jeans, either.

But suddenly she turned her head, said out of the complete blue, "We really do need a fence between our yards, to keep our pets separated."

"Yeah, you mentioned that before." Since she created the diversion, he was more than willing to embellish it. "Instead of a barrier kind of fence...what would you think about an electric one?"

"What a great idea. Then your dog and my dog can't cross over. But then it won't be an unfriendly fence. It'll just...you know. Help."

Exactly what he thought. Maybe their dogs didn't need it—but he sure as hell did. He needed something that would zap him—electrocute him if necessary—when he felt the urge to touch her again.

The electrocution idea seemed to gain momentum all on its own, because when he heard the sound of a car pulling in his drive, he jumped back from Amanda as if the foot between them was electrically charged.

The man climbing down from a tan SUV was a complete stranger. He was short and plump, sweating under his golf tan. He wore the usual suburban uniform of polo shirt and shorts, and approached them with a waxy smile and a hand raised to shake. "Hello. I live in the first house at the top of the cul-de-sac. I know you're Amanda Scott and Mike Conroy. I hope you both got a note from me when you first moved in."

If Mike had, he didn't remember it. Amanda did. "From the Home Owners' Association?"

"Yes, that's right."

"I thought it was nice of you to welcome a newcomer to the neighborhood that way," Amanda said warmly.

"I thought we'd better have a little talk before there were problems," Warren White said cordially.

"What problems?" Mike said warily.

"We have some rules in the neighborhood. Ordinances. Policies to keep the neighborhood to a standard we all like."

"Exactly what rules?" Mike's spine was instinctively stiffening. If this guy was going to try playing law games with him, he should have done his homework.

"I'm afraid you can't put a water garden in your backyard without permission."

"I beg your pardon?"

"And, Amanda, I'm afraid you need permission to plant trees, as well."

"What? You mean, the little dogwood I planted yesterday—?"

Warren kindly shook his head. "I'm afraid you needed permission. I'm sorry you didn't get it ahead of time."

Warren promised to put a list of the rules in each of their mailboxes. There were rules about what time a person could water their grass. Rules about recycling. Rules about noise. Rules about dandelion control. Rules about the length of grass allowed. Rules about no parking on the street overnight, no RV parking, no sheds put up in the yards—without permission. "Many people want fences, but we don't want the look of the neighborhood to deteriorate, so before putting in a fence, that's another thing you need to have permission for—"

"When exactly are these Home Owners' Association meetings, and where are they held?" Mike interrupted abruptly.

"Every third Thursday of the month. 7:00 p.m., after dinner. Because I'm president this year, I usually hold them in my family room. You're both welcome to attend. But I do assure you that the covenant rules are all legally binding."

For no apparent reason, Amanda suddenly snugged her hand in his, pressing hard, and stepped just a bit in front of him. "Thanks so much for stopping by, Mr. White. I suspect we're both likely to attend your next meeting. Thanks for filling us in."

When the superficial, supercilious jerk backed out of the driveway, she dropped his hand. "Okay. *Now* you can froth at the mouth. But try not to bellow at least until he's out of sight."

"Why would you think I was angry?"

"A wild guess," she assured him. "Although seeing you exhale fire was probably the first clue."

"Well, who elected him God? Did we suddenly land in a dictator state, or is this still America? What possible reason can there be why I can't have a water garden? And if he thinks I'm taking it out, he's about to find out why I made law partner when I was still in my twenties."

"Mike."

"What?"

"Try and remember that we're in a foreign country. I think they call it the suburbs."

Okay, okay, so she made him laugh in spite of himself.

And right then, Nancy and her George drove up—almost two hours earlier than planned. Teddy peeled out of the car faster than a criminal just granted parole.

Mike still wanted to finish his conversation with Amanda, but abruptly her hot-shot ex pulled in next door with Molly.

There was no more time to worry about sex or embraces or how damn much she was starting to mean to him.

From the look on his son's face, it was going to be a ticklish evening. And from the look on Molly's… Amanda was going to have her hands even more full.

* * *

Amanda didn't want to leave Mike. She knew the neighborhood "representative" had rubbed him the wrong way. Warren White struck her as the kind of ineffectual person who had no power in his real life, so he got a thrill out of imposing rules on others about their water-sprinkling schedules. Still, Mike should realize the guy was just a pompous wannabe bully... not a real problem.

In the meantime, though, she couldn't be the one to calm him down.

She definitely had her hands full with Molly.

Her daughter submitted to a bath, willingly changed into pink baby-doll pajamas, but after that, she folded her arms across her chest with a major diva scowl. "I want some mommy time and I want it *now*."

It wasn't as if Amanda hadn't been through this before. She put a fluffy blanket on the deck. Brought out the tray of nail polishes. Molly brought her doll-size tea set. The teapot was filled with milk.

"Daddy tricked me!" was the dramatic opening to Molly's tirade.

"How, honey?"

"He was real nice and real nice and real nice. Only, then we got to his house. And there was a lady there. A *stupid* lady."

Across the way, Amanda could see lights popping on and off at Mike's house. Her attention was on her daughter, but a thick clog seemed to have settled in her stomach. Mike was probably doing exactly what she was. Dealing with a child wounded by their divorce. Through no fault of their own, his Teddy and her Molly were both still reeling from the mistakes of their parents.

Molly, temporarily, stopped her rant to study her hands, which had been soaked and filed and were now ready for the fun part. Color. "Can we do our toenails after our hand nails?"

"Sure."

"I want yellow for my toenails."

"I'm pretty sure we have yellow." Amanda didn't actually look at the basket of polishes, but since color was always a major issue for her daughter, she was almost positive they had the whole crayon set of choices.

"And I want different colors for every hand nail."

"Okay." Amanda had learned a long time ago never to sweat the small stuff. "Now tell me more about your day."

"She had on this big fakey smile. Like grown-ups use for kids. And she says, 'How would you like to go shopping with me?' And I say, 'No, thanks, I'm here to see my dad.' And she says, 'If we go shopping, I thought I'd get you an American Girl doll.' And I say, 'No, thank you, my mommy gets me all the American Girl dolls I could possibly want.'" Molly looked up with stormy eyes. "Okay. So that was a lie. And it was really hard to say no, because I *really, really* need another American Girl doll. But she was being a pain."

"Honey. Sweetheart. Now, think a minute. It doesn't sound like she was being a pain. It sounds as if she was trying very, very hard to be nice to you."

"No. She just wanted to give me a doll so I'd like her. And I'm never going to like her. She had three boxes of games. And grape Kool-Aid. So fine. I played some games with her. But you know what?"

"What?" Amanda finished one of her daughter's hands, then started on the other.

"Daddy wasn't even *there* half the time. And he didn't play any games with me. But when he was there, you know what he did?"

"What, honey?"

"He and that lady took me to the back of the house, opened the door and said, 'Ta da!' And there was this room where I'm supposed to sleep when I'm there. It had a big white chair. And a big white bed. And shelves that already had books in them. And lots of stuffed animals all over the place."

Amanda felt her heart clutch. "It sounds very pretty."

Molly glowered at her mother. "I know it's pretty. That's not what was wrong. What was wrong is that *I don't sleep there.* Which I told them. Daddy said, 'But you will.' And the woman said, 'And when you come and stay with us, we want you to have your own special place.'"

Molly started blowing on both hands, trying to dry the polish faster. "I didn't say what I wanted to say. I remembered that I was supposed to be good, so I said, 'The room's real nice. Thank you.' And then I said, 'But I'm not sleeping over. Ever.' And you know what?"

"What, sweetheart?"

"The lady called me a brat. *Me. A brat!*"

"Oh, dear."

"So then I told her she was ugly. Which she is. And I said she must be stupid, too, because she couldn't even win at Candy Land. And she didn't even know to cut the crusts off my sandwich, either!"

Amanda had to zip her mouth closed. Obviously she couldn't say what she really wanted to, such as that she'd like to whack Thom upside the head—and that went double for The Bitch. She'd particularly like to tear out The Bitch's heart for trying to win over her daughter with material crap, and even more wanted to scream at her ex for not spending parenting time with his daughter himself.

But she couldn't just agree with Molly, because that would fuel her daughter's unhappiness with Thom.

So she just listened. And once they finished all the nail painting, she cuddled her daughter on the deck rocker until Molly was sleepy enough to fold into bed. Tomorrow, when the little one was less upset,

Amanda figured she'd think of some positive, constructive things to say about the day's debacle.

Tonight, she wasn't up for it.

For a half hour, she cleaned up toys, threw in a wash load, wiped down the kitchen. The whole time she was building up a good serious brood.

The whole evening had exemplified—painfully—why she had to quit playing attraction games with her next-door neighbor. The divorce was still fresh for her daughter. Molly had to be her one hundred percent primary concern. And just as relevant, Amanda knew perfectly well that her marriage, and divorce, established her stupid judgment about men.

There was no trusting her feelings for Mike. The magic, the pull, the wonder…that was the fairy tale. The wanting to believe there was a hero, a knight, a good man just for her. The wanting to believe in "in love."

The feeling that she was already *in* love with the damn man.

This was all exactly why she'd given up sex. Because she couldn't trust herself. Because she wanted her daughter to grow up seeing a strong, self-reliant mother…not a dependent female who couldn't get along without a man.

She had to *show* her daughter that she was strong, not just tell her.

Which meant she needed to just cool it with Mike. At least, for a much longer period of time.

That all settled in her mind, Amanda started turning out lights, closing up, locking the doors. When she climbed the stairs for bed, at the top stair she glanced out the window.

Night had fallen in a whisper of dew and stardust. Mike was upstairs, in his second-story window. He'd turned off his lights, too. He was probably enjoying just a few moments of peace and silence, probably no different than she was...but then he spotted her.

She could have moved. Could have waved. Could have...done pretty much anything.

But somehow heat transmitted across the driveways, through the closed windows, somehow past all the reasons she needed to get a serious brain.

She didn't just feel a pull toward him. She felt a force field.

He put a hand on his window.

Like a damn fool romantic idiot, she put a hand on her window.

And then, before she could do anything more stupid, she whipped around and headed straight, no talking, no thinking, no deterrents, to her bed. Alone. The way she needed to be.

Chapter Seven

Rain shivered down the windows, starting at day-break. Clouds bunched and punched, building into a dark gloomy morning even before breakfast. As Mike poured coffee, he studied his son.

Teddy had come home yesterday in a rare silent mood. He'd been contentious, crabby, couldn't settle in to play anything, wouldn't talk. Mike hadn't pushed him. Hell, the kid was as male as he was. Neither of them wanted to talk about *feelings*…but Mike figured a good night's sleep might help clear the air.

He'd set up the playing field to make talk easier. Let Teddy turn on cartoons—which Mike hated; he didn't like kids doing the whole veg-out-in-front-of-the-TV thing. But cartoons and scrambled eggs invariably brought out conversation, particularly when Teddy was allowed to eat in the living room.

His tough guy was curled up on the couch, still wearing his dinosaur pj's, Slugger glued to his side—a sure sign that Teddy was upset. Still, the kid had the remote. And a deep bowl of the scrambled eggs—this, because Mike had learned early on that the deeper the bowl, the less chance of spilled eggs all over the house.

Mike took the recliner with his plate and a mug of coffee. "So, hey. You never said anything about the zoo yesterday. You did go, didn't you?"

"Yeah."

"So, was it as fun as you thought it'd be?"

"It was fun for one whole second. Until George started sneezing and sneezing." Teddy, who rarely had power over the remote, was channel surfing at dizzying speeds. "He was the one who said he *wanted* to go. That was the thing. He kept saying we'd have fun. Only, he already *knew* he was 'lergic to animals."

Mike was already forming a wincer of a picture. "Okay. Then what happened?"

"We had to leave. That's what happened. Because he couldn't stop sneezing. But he said he'd make it up to me. We'd go to a nice place for lunch." Teddy froze on a different cartoon, then hit the trigger again.

"And?"

"And I thought he meant McDonald's. Chuck E. Cheese. Burger King. Someplace *good*. Instead it was this place where you had to wait and wait and wait. It had a tablecloth, and I didn't mean to pull it, but it was itching at my knees. So his drink got acc'dentally spilled. It wasn't my fault."

"What else happened?"

"We went back to their place. Mom played cards with me. Go Fish. Crazy Eights. Then I said, 'You wanna go swimming?' She said, 'Maybe another time.' I said, 'You wanna do a movie or something?' She said, 'Sure.' Only, she just turned on the TV. Not like going to a movie. And when she got a movie on, then she just left, started doing things. Talking on the phone. Talking to *him*. Cooking. Junk like that. Dad?"

When Teddy left the trigger at a news channel, Mike knew exactly how upset his tough guy was. "What, sport?"

"Mom doesn't want to be with me. She doesn't even like me. I want to be *here*. With you. All the time. I don't want to go with her anymore. And you know what else?"

"Tell me."

"George said I was rude. And he said I wasn't 'siplined."

'Siplined? Mike thought. "Disciplined?"

"That's what I *said*," Teddy said crossly. "And I said to mom on the way back, 'I don't get it. Why you're with him when you could be with Dad.' That's when he said I was rude."

Mike winced. "You asked your mom while he was right there in the car, huh?"

"Well, yeah. I didn't ask before. I wasn't thinking about it before. I asked her when I was thinking about it." Teddy put the bowl on the floor, then burrowed deeper into the cushions. Slugger burrowed after him. Cat suddenly leaped on the couch, looking fierce and lionlike. "This is how I like it, Dad. Us guys together. No more girls."

Mike remembered last night…whenever it was… when his house and Amanda's house were both closed down for the night, and he'd just stood at the window for a moment, inhaling the quiet…and there she was.

He wasn't touching her. Wasn't thinking about her. He'd been thinking about his kid. And her kid. And what divorces did to kids, and why he needed to get back to the Celibacy Principle. But then he'd looked at her and felt that…yearning.

Yearning to be with her.

To talk to her. To touch her. To hold her and be held.

This morning, of course, turned into another wake-up call. Yearning was just yearning. Sex was just sex. It wasn't the time. Period.

"Did you hear that?" Teddy grumbled.

"Yeah." Mike bounced up from the recliner, not certain if the sound was an actual knock on the back door—but something had provoked Slugger into going into his nose-to-the-sky warning bay. Of course, some days, a purr of a breeze could do that.

In this case, though, a pint-size rock star stood at the back door—at least Mike thought Molly's getup was about that. The sunglasses were unnecessary for a stormy morning, but the little shirt was full of glistening stars. Her red hair was all braided and pinned up with sequins or jewels or something. Her nails were painted like rainbows and her shoes had flashing lights.

At four years old, she had a petrifying amount of estrogen.

She might even be as bad as her mother in a few years.

Right then, though, he figured they had a more immediate problem on their plate. Molly was out of breath from running. Her lower lip was trembling, her big eyes spattering tears. "Mr. Mike. I need a punger. Right now. Right *right* now. For my mom!"

"A punger," Mike said blankly.

"A punger! You know! A punger!" Quickly she said, "*Please!* This is *serious!*"

"A punger," Mike repeated, but then he got it. Plunger. Plumbing problems. Some kind of major uh-oh. "Tell your mom I'll be right there."

"It needs to be *now.*"

"I understand, Molly. I just need to get a tool kit and the plunger."

"But don't tell mommy I told you. She told me to

sit in the living room, that she could handle it. But there was water *everywhere*. And she was saying bad words. I'd tell you what the words were, but I can't say them. My mommy says that nobody says those words in her house. Or my house. My mom—"

"Okay, honey. We're going to stop talking now, and start moving." He pushed on shoes, then grabbed tools, locked up the baying Slugger and herded Teddy out with him. He suspected Amanda might just guess that someone had "told" on her—particularly when he showed up with a plunger and tools—but that wasn't remotely relevant.

Keeping his hands off her was one issue.

Not helping her if she was in trouble was completely different.

He yelled a hello when he opened her back door. "Oh, it's you, Mr. Mike!" said the rock star in her loudest voice. She was still wearing the shades. "What a surprise! It's Mr. Mike, Mom!"

"Molly Ann! Did you go next door and—"

"Me?" But to Mike, she lifted her head and whispered, "I'm in trouble."

"I'll fix that. You and Teddy either play or watch some TV for a little while, okay?"

It wasn't hard to locate Amanda. The place had deteriorated since he saw it last. There seemed to be a whole bunch more purples and pale blues. Pillows. More pillows. Stuff to run into, stuff on top of tables. Flowers all over the place. But the main downstairs bathroom—where the descriptive vocabulary was coming from—had water seeping into the hall.

She must have heard him set down the tool kit, because she started talking—even though she hadn't wasted a second turning around. "Go away, Mike. I can fix my own problems! I am not looking for someone to save me every time I get into some stupid mess!"

"Okay."

"This would *not* be a good time to laugh."

"Okay."

"Don't say one word! I mean it! Just go back home!"

Weeellll. He couldn't quite say okay to that. The bathroom had definitely been redefined since his last visit. Now it seemed to be covered in butterflies. Butterfly wallpaper, butterfly pictures, butterfly toilet seat, towels embroidered with butterflies. It was almost enough to give a guy a rash—if he'd had the time to itch.

Amanda was pretty wet. Knees, feet, clothes. Towels had been used to sop up the water—or some of it. A few rolls of paper towels had been used for the same purpose. At some point she'd had a book open—*Basic Plumbing Repairs*—but that likely wasn't helping her a whole lot at this point, because it was like learning to sail after your boat had already capsized.

"I do *not* want advice. Don't you say one word!"

"I won't, I won't." He was still trying to evaluate the situation. Not the plumbing problem. Her. Amanda was the only problem that mattered. She wasn't crying, exactly. At least there were no sissy, sad tears leaking down her cheeks. This was more…a major, furious, sputtering type of crying.

He said carefully, "Behind the toilet is a shutoff valve."

"You think I didn't know that?" She huffed. *"Where?"*

"Just behind there. Look. You'll see it. Turn it off—against the clock. If it's too tight or hard to move, I could—"

"Do not touch anything. *I will do* it. And don't tell me any more, either!"

"Okay." It was amazing…almost from the minute he'd met her, he'd been tensed up. It was that relentless attraction thing. But now, finally, he could relax. He didn't have to worry about falling in love with her anymore. She was a shrew. A witch times ten. She had a completely unreasonable and irrational side.

"Do we know what went down the toilet that shouldn't have?" he asked delicately.

"An American Girl doll shoe."

"A doll's shoe," he repeated.

"Possibly both shoes. She was dressing the doll when she went potty. Now the shoes are gone. And right after she left the bathroom, this all—" she motioned "—started."

"Okay. Now, has the toilet run before? I mean, constantly run?"

"I just moved in this house. It was new, but not brand-new. Is there some reason in the *universe* I should know that answer for sure?"

"No, no," he said in his best tiptoe voice. "It's just that the more we know, the better chance we have of understanding the whole problem."

"*I'm* the *only* one who has to understand *anything*."

"You're so right." Hell, his pulse was practically humming. At the moment, she was as easy to love as a stingray. A splotchy-cheeked, furious, unmanageable stingray. "Amanda, I don't know if you have an auger, but I happened to bring one over. I wasn't going to use it myself. But you could. If you wanted to."

"I don't even know what a flipping auger is! Go home, Mike!"

"I'm going. I promise. In just a second. I just want to show you the auger... See? On one end, it has a corkscrew. So you push that end down into the hole... then you turn the handle—clockwise—until the entire spring has been fed into the pipe as far as it'll go. The idea is to reach the obstruction..."

She tried. The first time she didn't quite get it, and shot him a look filled with venom. Probably snake venom.

"I won't offer to do it, I swear," he promised, hands in the air. "It's just...you could try it again. In fact, you could try it a couple of times. If you wanted to. And when this is all over, you might want to put some ice on that elbow."

"I'm not hurt."

"I'm sorry. I didn't mean to say anything nice. It just slipped out…and yeah, you've got it now. That's the how of it. So when the auger's all the way in, you could try—only if you want to!—to slowly, slowly pull the spring back. If that doesn't free up the doll's shoe, you could try it a second time."

Thank God it worked. Out came a little white shoe. Amazing how much trouble a shoe less than two inches long could cause a person in life.

She started breathing a little better. Not a *lot* better. But definitely an improvement over the hyperventilating, crying, fire-breathing dragon she'd been a half hour ago.

"Okay now. I'm leaving. I'm going to take a wild guess that you don't have an indoor-outdoor vac—why would you? So I'll just bring mine over, leave it on your deck. It should suck up this water in no time. But before I leave…maybe you might want to turn on the water again. Remember? The shutoff valve? This time you turn it the other way."

"I hear patronizing in your voice."

"I swear. There isn't a patronizing thought in my head." His tone probably sounded virtuous because he was telling the complete truth. There was nothing on his mind but fear. He just wanted to get out of the house alive.

When she did the shutoff-valve thing and the crisis was finally completely over—except for the cleanup—she started crying again.

This time, he just backed away. There was a time to hold a woman. And a time when a man knew he'd sure as hell better get out of Dodge.

He was in bare feet by then, but he picked up his sandals by the back door, went searching for Teddy and Molly. The two were lying on the floor, leaned up on their elbows, watching TV. Only not cartoons. They were watching a mother give live birth. Apparently the event had just happened.

"Holy mother of…" Mike got calm, fast. In three long strides, he grabbed the remote, clicked off the TV and set it high on the mantel. "Molly. Do yourself a *big favor* and don't tell your mother what you were just watching. You can tell her another day. Just not today."

"I won't, Mr. Mike. Princess and Darling and me are going stay out of Mommy's way for a while."

"Good. Teddy. With me."

"But, Dad. Did you see all that blood? Wasn't it gross? Can we watch it at our house?"

"Zip it, Theodore. Not one word until we're back in our own house. Not *one*. Not even a little one. You have no idea how serious I am."

"Me, too, Dad," his son assured him. "I'm *really* serious."

Mike wanted to laugh…and then did. When a day started out this rough, it could only go up—because it sure couldn't get any worse.

The morning couldn't possibly get worse, Amanda was sure. But of course it did. The bathroom was still going to take hours to clean up, and Darling had an appointment with the vet at 10:00 a.m.

And then, out of the blue, her mother showed up. Gretchen regarded the whole plumbing mess, offered to hire a cleaning service to immediately come and take care of it, and that caused an argument. It wasn't a *bad* argument, or a mom-daughter sniping event, nothing like that. It was just that her mother couldn't hear a "No, thank you" with a megaphone.

Eventually Gretchen mentioned the reason for her visit—she wanted to take Molly swimming. That was totally a *good* thing, except that it took time to get gear together for an afternoon at a pool. And her mom was barely out the door before the phone rang.

It was her attorney, who wanted a meeting related to Thom's filing for joint custody. That wasn't exactly *bad*. She wanted to be prepared for the court date. It was just that any thought of Thom's sharing custody put a worried dent in her heart.

As if the morning didn't have enough complications, she'd barely finished with the floor and had a first load of towels and rags in the washer when there was a knock at the front door. A large truck had backed into her driveway. All the heavy things she'd ordered were being delivered—from the bricks to the patio stones, to the shiny green riding lawn mower.

The delivery guys took nearly an hour—but Amanda's mood brightened immediately.

It was the lawn mower. She'd almost forgotten about it. Her parents hadn't moved to the suburbs until she was in college; she'd just never been exposed to lawn-care issues. But now, the machine immediately made her think of Mike.

Ever since he'd come over that morning—and damn him, been a hero for her yet *again*—she'd wanted to gallop over there and heartily apologize. Only, darn it, it wasn't that simple. It was probably a good thing that something happened to force distance between them.

He'd seen her at her worst. That was good. It'd stop him from looking at her with those...well, with those eyes. Those eyes that communicated that he thought her damned incredible. Not just attractive, but compelling. Interesting. That he valued being with her. That he went crazy when he touched her.

So. Possibly her behaving like the witch of the universe was a secret godsend. But the lawnmower was another godsend—because it would give her the chance to make up.

Once the delivery man left, she sat on the lawnmower seat with a coffee mug and the instruction manual. Then turned her new baby on. A few stripped gears later, and she had the hang of it…or she would, once she got the speed thing under control.

Her mood moved from low to a reasonable soar. She didn't need a man to do work. Just because she wasn't mechanical didn't mean that she couldn't learn—or teach her daughter to learn.

She'd show Mike competence. She'd *be* competent. He didn't have to know what it was all about—how desperately she wanted to change, how much she never wanted to lean on a man again. Maybe plumbing crises were never going to be her thing, but this adorable riding mower was downright fun.

She finished her lawn, which she had to admit, represented a little learning curve. A few spots were higher than other spots. She'd sort of bumped a couple of trees. There was one small strip of grass in the front yard that she'd sort of missed. But she'd learned. And now she headed next door.

His yard was bigger than hers, but simpler. Naturally she wasn't going anywhere near the water-garden construction site, but he had a long, long backyard. For once, she was doing something for *him*. Not just making up for being a bitch this morning…but actually doing something nice. Decent. Something a friend would do.

Best yet, he was gone—so he'd come home

to a freshly mowed lawn—and not even know it was her.

She was within a few swipes of finishing in the front, when her brand-new baby started coughing. Then sputtering. Then gave out a death sigh and just plain stopped.

She'd run out of gas.

Chapter Eight

When Mike pulled into the driveway around two o'clock, Teddy's mood shifted from cranky and whiny to ecstatic. His four-year-old hadn't appreciated his first visit to the dentist, even though they'd done a fast-food lunch and a romp in the park afterward.

"It still hurts, Dad," Teddy whined, as he unsnapped his seat belt. But then he saw the tractor. That was the last Mike heard about the dentist. Now it was all, "Oh, wow, oh, wow, oh, wow!"

Mike may have climbed from the pickup more slowly, but his son's oh-wow opinion echoed his own. Certainly he'd never seen the behemoth of a lawn mower parked in his front yard before.

"We don't climb on equipment that isn't ours,

Teddy," he admonished. But hey, he couldn't resist doing a leisurely stroll around the thing, giving it a thump and pat and an admiring general look-see. Slugger ambled out of the dog door to greet them—well, mostly to greet Teddy. The hound hadn't appreciated having his man parts clipped at the vet's, and he was still letting Mike know about it. Still, all three boys slowly circled the machine with equal reverence.

"Is it ours, Dad?"

"No."

"Why not? If it's in our yard? Whose is it?"

"I don't know. But I'm pretty sure I can make a good guess."

"Maybe I could just sit in the seat for a second."

"Maybe we never do that without the permission of the owner."

Mike wanted to shake his head. Not at his son. At the mower. It was a John Deere. A beauty. One of the X700 series. Forty-eight-inch mower deck. Color-coded buttons, cruise control, CD player, four-wheel steering.

It was the kind of riding mower that a landscaping company owned. Or maybe a golf course. Not that Mike knew much about tractors, but he was pretty sure this one checked in at several thousand. No one—that is, no one normal—would buy such a thing for a regular-size yard that he could imagine. So that was the first clue to its owner.

The second clue was that *his* yard had been mowed. It would recover, of course. Grass always grew back.

The third clue was when he figured out why it was sitting in his yard. It had run out of diesel.

Add it all up, and Mike glanced next door…only to see Amanda bouncing into her drive. She pelted out of the car, popped the lid on the trunk. "Hi, guys!" she called out. "I'll get the mower out of there! Would you believe it? I ran out of fuel! So I had to run to the gas station, but I've got it, I've got it—"

"Miss Amanda? Can I sit on it? Can I?"

"Yes, honey—but *only* if your dad or I'm there. Okay? No one else can give you permission but us."

"Okay. I love you," Teddy mentioned, and that was the end of his talking to her. Amanda kind of stopped dead when he said the word *love,* but instead of looking at his son, her eyes shot straight up to his.

Mike's response was identical. To make eye contact that instant. It was one of those rare mind-meld moments. As if they were the only two people in the universe who realized there was an avalanche big enough to destroy them all. Maybe no one else saw it. But they did. Maybe no one else had a clue. But they did.

All morning he'd tried to reassure himself that he wasn't falling. It should have helped that she'd been as unreasonable as a shrew with PMS that morning. But it hadn't.

After a morning of major plumbing messes, apparently lawn mowing, then running out of diesel, Amanda was still Amanda. Her scoop-neck top had grass stains; her shorts looked almost wrinkled... but they matched. Pale blue and dark blue. Her hair hadn't seen a brush in a while, which meant it was like copper on fire in the sunlight, pretty wild...but she still had on lip gloss, cute sandals, earrings.

She almost fell under the weight of the diesel can, but she managed to pluck it out of the trunk, her smile fifty times more powerful than a kilowatt. "You don't have to thank me," she chattered on. "I owed you, for all the stuff you've done for me. I was totally happy to find something I could do the other way around! I just didn't realize how much fuel it would take to mow both yards. Or how much fuel they put in to start with. And it took me a little while to figure out how to run it. I've never mowed grass before! Would you believe it?!"

He believed it. It just didn't seem wise to agree with her, much less while she was still struggling with the fuel container. "You want me to do that for you?"

"No, no sweat, I can do it!"

"Amanda."

"Huh?"

He tried to make his voice sound light and conversational and delicate—although possibly he was incapable of managing "delicate." "Who sold you this mower?"

"Oh. The hardware store. The guy was wonderful. Seriously. Gave me exactly what I asked for."

He aimed for the same ultralight tone. "And you asked for...?"

"I told him that I only wanted to buy one mower in a lifetime, so for sure I didn't want junk. And I wanted one with power, because I'm not particularly physically strong. I wanted quality, serious dependability, nothing that I'd have trouble servicing..."

Okay, he was beginning to see how she'd gotten in so much trouble. She'd asked good questions. She'd just asked the wrong salesperson. "Did he ask you what size yard you have?"

"Sure. But it's not as if I had the exact dimensions. I just told him straight. *Big.*" She shot him another grin, as she finished feeding diesel into the mower and screwed the top back on. Suddenly, though, her smile faded. "Why all the questions? Do you think I made a bad choice?"

She'd made a terrible choice. It wasn't just the money, but that it was way too much machine for what she needed. But suddenly that wasn't the point. Her breathtaking smile had completely disappeared now, and in its place was a look of uncertainty... fragility.

In a flash, he realized he'd seen that look of raw

uncertainty before. This morning. In between moments when she'd more or less been chewing him up, no matter what he said. Still. There'd been glimpses of That Look.

He remembered her saying more than once that she'd been raised as a spoiled, sheltered princess.

But he hadn't added it up before. How much she'd been life-crippled by her background, and how much that bothered her. The basic practical information most people knew, she just plain didn't. Common sense wasn't common, not the way she was raised. And she was trying. Watching her with the plunger and the "Dare To Repair" book that morning... watching her in the hardware store, picking out tools, painting on her own, and yeah, now, diving into the mechanics of lawn mowing and mowers.

"What?" she said impatiently. "You think I didn't pick the right machine?"

"I think you're brilliant. That you picked the best."

The shoulders eased. The smile went back to being shiny and disarming...and sexy. "Well. I know I didn't know what I was doing. But I tried to ask the right questions—"

"You're going to be the envy of the neighborhood."

"I don't care about that. But I can do this. My lawn. Your lawn. That kind of maintenance. There's no reason I should have to ask for help. Or hire it out."

He didn't look back at the butcher job. And if anyone else made a remark to her, well, he'd just have to kill them.

As if suddenly realizing he wasn't the center of attention, Teddy edged forward and said to Amanda, "Guess what? I went to the dentist this morning. For the first time in my whole life. The dentist let me squirt the water. It was really cool."

Mike stared at his son, astonished at Teddy's volunteering such a creative version of this morning's events. But then, men seemed genetically programmed to reinvent certain events or truths, if it meant impressing a female they cared about.

Damn. It was getting harder and harder to deny it. It wasn't just his son who cared. Mike was sinking in deeper and thicker than quicksand. He just didn't know what to do about it.

Clouds bunched in fists. Thunder grumbled, bringing on another session of wild, slashing rain. Amanda glanced next door as she raced to the car.

She'd barely seen Mike in the past two weeks, except in passing.

They waved when they saw each other. One morning, Teddy had popped in to ask for a couple of eggs. One afternoon, she'd sent Molly next door with a fresh strawberry-rhubarb pie.

She'd mowed his lawn. He'd sent over quotes for electric fences.

She'd sent a response to his fence quotes. One night, Thom had stopped by—to fight about custody, naturally—and she'd stepped out on the deck so Molly wouldn't hear the heated words. Across the way, she'd seen Mike choose that time to put a foot up on his deck—he was ostensibly holding a bottle of beer, but she had no doubt he'd have charged over if Thom had gotten out of hand.

She was invisibly watching over him, too. For instance, she'd bandaged Teddy's knee when she'd seen his son take a tumble on the concrete drive.

They were taking care of each other—and avoiding each other at the same time. That couldn't go on forever, obviously, but as far as Amanda could tell, they were both being smart. Why stroll in woods that was filled with poison ivy?

She turned the windshield wipers on full, glanced at her GPS, tried to take her mind off Mike. Her father had kidnapped Molly for a day at the Fields Museum, so storms or no storms, she needed to take advantage of the free time. June was sneaking into July. She'd already researched preschools and pediatricians, but she wanted to do an eyes-on before committing to either for sure.

Ten minutes later, she parked in front of Denise and Dan's Play School—and got half soaked just running the few steps from the car. Sandals squeaking, hat dripping, she opened the shiny red door. Naturally she'd called ahead to tour the facility. Dan—the dad of the D&D team—was waiting for her. His easy smile was the first thing that won her over. Everything about him—and the place—radiated a love and understanding for little ones.

She loved what she saw. There was a music room, a plant room, a "critter" room—a place where live animals were either borrowed or housed, from aquariums to turtles and spiders and hamsters. The last door on the right was clearly an art room, where smocks hung on hooks, and the walls were exuberantly finger painted.

The bathrooms were spotless, the facilities all miniature-sized—yet there were also high shelves that stocked underpants and other emergency replacement clothing in a variety of sizes. A central room included a locked refrigerator, where milk and fruits were stored. Available snacks were listed, fruits, nut bars, no cookies allowed except for special occasions.

A gigantic bathtub, near a window, was piled high with pillows and blankets. "Not for naps," Dan explained. "But kids sometimes get stomachaches. Or just want to curl up and have some quiet time. When a four-year-old gets out of control, our philosophy is…of course, to remove them from the situation and give them a chance to control themselves. But before we make that into a penalty, we try the curl-up in the tub thing. Most of the time, a child wants to get under control. They just don't know how yet. So…"

He opened the front door for her, still talking. Outside, rain still sluiced down, turning green leaves emerald and putting a sting of freshness in the air. She reached in her jacket pocket for her hat, still listening to Dan, but trying to hurry along now. "So you need me to let you know within the next couple of weeks."

"That would be best. We're almost booked up now—"

"Well, it's yes, I can tell you right now. I'd have brought the checkbook if I'd known for sure what a terrific facility you have."

She turned around, stepped down, and...*wham*. Another burst of thunder and lightning startled her— not coming from the skies, but from Mike.

He was headed up at the same time she was headed down. Their eyes met, and there it was, the chemistry of the century. Even with her hair frizzing up and her face washed of makeup, she felt conscious of her breasts, her pelvis. Her skin, the beat in her throat.

The preschool owner was still talking, as if he had no clue Armageddon was taking place on his school steps. Mike smiled, slow and easy, but he was still taking a lazy sip of how she looked, and she was drinking in his damp hair and sassy eyes and long, lanky frame just as zealously.

Naturally, she got a grip. "You're checking out the preschool?"

"Yeah. Been making the rounds all morning."

She gave him a thumbs-up, to show him her vote on the facility, but Dan immediately engaged him in conversation, so she had every excuse to continue on her way.

There, she thought. Both of them had managed that beautifully. Easy. Comfortable with each other—but neither risking a step closer to harm's way.

Maybe Amanda wasn't strong, but she was getting stronger. Maybe she hadn't learned self-confidence yet, but she was getting there, too. She was coping. She was making a life. She was being the best mom she knew how to be.

She just had to refrain from jumping down any well pits.

Okay, Mike kept telling himself. So he'd run into her checking out preschools. That wasn't so odd. Certainly not prophetic. They both had four-year-olds. They'd both just moved. They both had a lot of parenting things to do.

Besides…preschools weren't sexy. Parenting wasn't sexy, either.

It was in his head. That she belonged with him. That he belonged with her.

He had to get it out of his head. He was too damned old—and smart—to let his hormones do his thinking.

Stopped at a red light, he glanced again at the address. In another minute, he'd be at Dr. June Weavers, who was one of the five pediatricians he'd researched. He could still take Teddy into Chicago—it's not as if they lived hundreds of miles away from his original pediatrician. But it made no sense, to trek a sick kid on freeways and through rush hours. Finding a closer doctor was the more logical option.

It finally stopped raining after lunch, but the sky was still drizzling. The trees looked waxed-wet and shiny, but humidity hung in the air like a blanket. He parked, noting the expensive landscaping at the doctors' complex, took the stairs up two at a time.

And paused.

Amanda had just pushed through the door and was bolting down the steps. She'd have barreled straight into him if he hadn't put out a hand.

The simple touch made her head shoot up. She sucked in a breath before she found a wry smile. "Pretty unbelievable, huh? Two places in a row?" And then, "Don't waste your time. This one's a no vote."

"Really?"

She listed her concerns. "Four crying kids in the waiting room. The receptionist was frazzled and out of patience. Dust in the corners. Just...no."

"The doctor had hefty credentials."

"I thought so, too. And maybe she's brilliant. But it's just not a well-run place."

"You have more on your pediatrician list?"

She nodded. "Oh, yeah. Dr. Alan Rivers is the next on mine—"

"He was at the top of my choices, but I was doing a circle, hitting the geographically closest ones first."

"Well…"

"Well…"

Since they both had cars, it seemed a foolish idea to leave one, but they both liked the idea of checking out "Dr. Alan" together. Two sets of eyes were always better than one. The office was just five blocks from the first doctor—but a major difference in worlds.

Mike stalled in the waiting room. The setting was a kid's dream. A big-screen TV carried a whole selection of programs, from reading shows to movies like *Free Willy*. An aquarium took almost a whole width of wall, with all sorts of colorful fish darting around, the setup no higher than his knees. There was a lot for a kid to do besides wait and worry, he thought.

Amanda tracked down Dr. Alan for both of them. The doctor emerged from the exam rooms as soon as he was free. The guy was almost as little as his patients, big glasses, floppy hair, a bright blue stethoscope. Amanda remarked on the bins near the doorway—a child could pick out a pair of slippers, if he or she wanted to wear them in the office. And another bin held small, washable stuffed animals. A sign read Pick a Friend to Take in the Room with You.

The doctor gave them a full ten minutes. Neither

needed more. On the way out, Amanda said, "For me, this is a cut-and-dried. He's my guy."

"Because the place was so kid-friendly?"

"Yeah. That mattered. And it was spotless. And no one was in uniform."

"And nobody looked scared."

She smiled at him. "Yeah. That was the biggie. I don't doubt kids cry when they're getting a vaccine, but I liked it, that none of the kids looked afraid, even though they were at the doctor's."

His truck was parked next to her car, where both of them hesitated again. "So we've got two things marked off the parenting list for the day?" he asked.

"Yup. And I'm exhausted."

He laughed. "You think there's a chance we can refrain from running into each other for a few hours?"

She stopped smiling, cocked her head. Something passed between them—something that muted the sounds of traffic and voices, that intensified the rustle of wet leaves and hint of lilac in the air. Something that made her eyes look mesmerizingly honest. That made him want to look and never stop looking.

"I'm not sure we're going to manage it," she said suddenly, softly.

"Manage what?"

"Staying out of trouble."

She turned around, ducked in her car. He stood

there even after she'd backed out of the parking lot and zoomed down the street.

He was about eighty-eight percent sure that she'd just given him a dare. She hadn't *said,* "I want trouble." But her tone had a whispery dare in it. Her eyes had a fever-bright dare for damn sure. Her body, her smiles… Oh, yeah. She was all about danger and dares.

It wasn't a good idea to dare a guy who was at the end of his hormonal tether. He'd been good as gold. But like his four-year-old said—his *male* four-year-old—nobody could be good *all* the time.

Amanda arrived at Warren White's house at ten to seven. As she'd expected, the White decorating scheme was beige. As in, beige, period. No bright color had seen a surface in the White house. The setup for the Home Owners' Association meeting was a gathering in Warren's great room…which opened onto a deck, where teenagers were supposed to watch over the little kids who came with their parents. Amanda wasn't about to trust strangers with Molly, but she could see there were a ton of kids there, all having fun.

Still, she sat next to the door, with an eye on the yard outside. The older kids started a game of Mother, May I…and Molly, being the competitive tiny overachiever that she was, instantly joined in.

Amanda relaxed—a little—and scoped the room,

trying to pick up names, friendly faces, who had which kids of what ages. She'd worn a scoop-neck top with white slacks, sandals, just a scrunchie pulling her hair back…while she knew the dress code for a city job with her hands tied behind her back, she wasn't so sure of the rules in the suburbs. Most seemed to take her in as "one of them" from the start—a relief.

At least until Mike walked in.

Warren took center stage in front of his fireplace precisely at 7:00 p.m. He even had a little gavel. Cute, she thought. Pompous and silly, but still kind of cute.

Mike wasn't. The women all silenced when he walked in—Amanda suspected they hadn't seen that much testosterone in one package in a *long* time. He'd brushed and showered, done the whole cleanup thing, but he still had that look—the cross between ruffian and quarterback. He was a bad boy with charm. They could all smell it.

He spotted her in less than a millisecond. And there it was again. The Dare. Just like this afternoon. She'd been a perfect lady, hadn't done a thing to entice or invite him, had been keeping to her celibacy pledge like a damned saint.

But at the preschool, then the pediatricians' offices…well. He'd been daring her, Amanda thought darkly. And he was still daring her. She'd *tried* to be honest with him. She'd *tried* to stay out of his way, to avoid temptation, to just be a good neighbor and a good friend. But he had to quit looking at her that way. Had to quit sending out those hungry, hungry vibes…as if he wanted to eat her up, and to spend a whole long night doing it.

He was sending out dares.

As if she'd sucker into that childish double-dog-dare kind of thing. Well, she was smarter than that. She smiled at him, crossed her legs at the ankles, went for the ladylike posture. *She* wasn't the one who was asking for trouble. It was him. Every time he looked at her. Every time he came close. Every time he breathed.

"Calling the meeting of the Home Owners' Association to order. Lucy, would you read the minutes from the May meeting?"

Warren started the meeting in a voice that resembled the drone of flies in the summer. Lucy—a woman with cotton-candy hair and a girl's swim-team logo—dutifully read the minutes.

Mike quietly crossed the room to sit next to her. Since Teddy wasn't with him, she glanced outside— and yeah, there he was, already teamed up next to Molly in the crowd of kids in the big backyard. The game had changed to "Simon Says." The kids looked happy.

She wasn't.

For a man who had almost no hips and no butt, somehow he took up a huge amount of room. He smelled like fresh soap and vanilla ice cream. And yearning. He definitely smelled like yearning. He carried a folder.

"New business," Warren announced.

Mike raised his hand.

"Well. It's nice to have a newcomer so willing to participate in our group. Welcome, Mr. Conroy."

"Mike," he said as he stood up.

There followed a gasper.

She knew the neighbor who raised worms for his kid, who dug in mud, who neglected to shave for days at a time. But she didn't know the lawyer. She'd never have guessed Mike could turn into a powerhouse who tapped into authority and command the minute he opened his mouth.

He was wearing sandals, for Pete's sake.

He didn't talk for long, just said he wanted to respond to issues raised by his putting in a water garden in his backyard...and a proposed electric fence he wanted to install. He handed a legal-looking document to Warren, but to the group of home owners, he laid out the gist of it more simply.

"I didn't realize the Home Owners' Association had 'rules' until Warren expressed them to me. My response is that document. I guarantee that I'll return the property to its original condition, if or when I sell the place. I also guarantee that the water garden I've been putting in will exceed any standard of good landscaping set by your association..."

There was quite a bit more. When he finally sat down again, Warren had the expression of a major suck-up. "Mike, Mike, Mike. None of us were objecting to the water garden. We think it's a wonderful idea. We just wanted you—and anyone else who's new to the neighborhood—to *ask* first."

When the meeting was over, the group of neighborhood women swarmed Mike. Amanda might have gotten a cup of lemonade with the rest…except that her mom's ear, the left one, picked up the sound of crying.

Not her Molly's crying.

But Teddy.

Chapter Nine

Mike would have chosen to stay a few more minutes at the infamous Home Owners' Association, partly to shake hands with a few more neighbors—but mostly to walk home with Amanda. But Teddy's brouhaha forced an immediate exit.

Teddy held his hand on the short walk home. He didn't talk. Couldn't. There were no tears now, but his eyes were still blotchy, his mood still stormy. Teddy didn't want to cry in public. Mike understood that guy kind of pride.

Once at home, though, Mike lifted him to the kitchen counter, plucked ice cream from the freezer, got them both spoons. "So just say. What happened."

"There was this stupid girl."

"Yeah, when I was your age, a lot of stories started that way." There were more ice cream cartons in the freezer than meat. Mike pulled the cover off the Cherry Vanilla. One spoonful for Teddy. Two for him.

"We were doing Simon Says. And I took four steps like I was supposed to, only that meant I sort of ran into this stupid girl. So she turned around and slugged me."

Mike did the next round of ice cream, this time with a wet dishcloth ready for the spill he knew was coming.

"I didn't *do* anything, Dad. I was just playing the game like I was supposed to. Only, I won the last one and I think she didn't like that. When she punched me, I really, really, really, *really* wanted to punch her back. But I didn't. You tole me a million times. You never hit a girl."

"You did the right thing," Mike assured him. "So then what?"

"So Molly hit her."

"Molly?"

"That was the thing. I told her I couldn't hit a girl. She said fine, but nobody ever said she couldn't. So she hit her. But, Dad. It's a bad thing. A very bad thing. When a girl has to do your hitting for you. I was so mad I started crying. It wasn't *fair.*"

Mike put away the ice cream, hooked his arms to

make a seat for his big guy, and they moved into the bathroom, then the bedroom. Slugger and Cat both knew Teddy was upset. The critters climbed on the bed first, so there was almost no room for Teddy.

Mike was still trying to figure out what had upset Teddy more—that a strange girl had hit him, or that Molly had been his hero instead of his having the chance to be one himself.

Apparently his stress level wasn't all that great, because he zonked out before Mike could pull up the covers or turn out the light. "Cat. Slugger," he called, thinking that the critters needed one more let-out that night…but neither acknowledged him in any way.

They weren't leaving the kid.

Abruptly the house turned silent…and Mike turned restless. He cleaned up in the kitchen, because he'd learned early on that ice cream spills were easier to deal with when they happened, rather than waiting for the next day. After that…well, there was always stuff to do. Start a load of wash. Hit the mail, go through bills.

Instead, he just…sort of aimlessly paced. Overall, he wasn't unhappy at how the Home Owners' meeting had gone. He'd gotten what he wanted. He just had a real bug about other people imposing rules on him…but most of the neighbors were nice enough. A bunch of the guys invited him to a Wednesday-night poker game. A few moms had clustered around him, talking about preschools.

But the only one he'd wanted to be with was Amanda. He wanted to know what she thought of the group. He wanted to tease her—she was supposed to be as afraid of suburbia as he was—yet she'd fit in so easily; both men and women warmed to her right away. Not that he was surprised. She gave off a quiet friendliness, an honesty and warmth.

His prowling around eventually led him to his front window, where he just stood there, staring at the windows in her place. Her household looked shut down. Molly had undoubtedly been put to bed by now. He saw no movement in any of the rooms, nothing but some distant light.

She definitely wasn't finishing her evening on the deck tonight. The firefly-night rolled through his mind on slow replay. The fireflies, the dancing in the grass, the moonlight, her soft silver laugher... He remembered every minute of that crazy evening.

Abruptly realizing how long he'd been standing there, staring at empty windows next door like a complete fool, he pivoted around. Kicked off his shoes. Headed for the shower.

When Molly was finally asleep, Amanda left her daughter's bedroom with a major sigh. They'd had quite a discussion before bedtime—brought on by the shiner in her daughter's left eye. It wasn't a bad bruise, considering the other little girl in the altercation had been a hefty second grader. But it invoked a torrent of talk about when "wrong is wrong" and when "wrong is right."

It was always wrong to fight, Molly knew.

But it was always right to stand up for a friend against a bully.

So which was the rightest answer? If you had to act really quick and your friend was hurt *right then* and there was no time to go in and ask your mom?

Amanda wasn't about to agree that hitting was an effective answer for anything, but by the time she wandered into the kitchen, her head was spinning. In the next life, she wanted to be her daughter. So passionate about life. So full of spirit and love and absolutely certain of what she felt about everything.

Without turning on a light, Amanda opened the fridge, then a cupboard. There didn't seem to be anything she wanted to eat or drink. Nothing she wanted to do. She was definitely too antsy to watch a show or read…and positively too wide-awake to sleep.

But then she froze.

Mike was awake. She could see him across the way, a tall dark silhouette. The distant sink light provided the only illumination, or she'd never have caught his shadowed frame. He couldn't see her. He was facing her windows, but she had no lights on. So it was unlikely he could see her, yet he stood there, as if he were searching, and then suddenly turned away and disappeared back into the darkness.

Her pulse started thrumming…and wouldn't

stop. A lump filled her throat…that refused to be swallowed.

It was his loneliness that struck her. An invisible loneliness, nothing he'd say or admit to, nothing anyone was supposed to see.

But he'd been looking at her house, her windows. For *her*. Even if he never said it. Even if he never intended to do anything about it.

And something abruptly snapped in Amanda. She couldn't explain what exactly. She just felt suddenly, oddly…angry. Vibrantly angry. Impatiently, infuriatingly, zestily angry.

She tore around the house faster than a wet cat, brushing her hair, brushing her teeth, unearthing the monitor she used when Molly was a baby. Then she charged outside, barefoot, prancing fast because the grass was wet and the night damp-cool and ghostly.

Before she lost her nerve—before she got scared—she zipped up his deck steps, didn't knock on the back door, just pushed open the glass and charged in. Immediately she stubbed her toe—on heaven knows what, probably a toy—made a groan of a sound, loud enough to wake the dead, but his watchdog didn't even come out to see her, much less bark. Mike couldn't possibly be sleeping yet; she'd seen him from the window less than ten minutes ago. But he didn't show up, either, no matter how much noise she was making, stomping around.

Of course she realized why, when she aimed

toward a flicker of light, and finally heard the sound of water coming from the master bath.

She took a step into his bedroom, and in the dark, for just a second, she lifted her foot because the toe was still stinging. She was acting crazily, she knew. She was behaving completely out of character.

She was taking a risk she was terribly afraid of.

On paper, this was just an impossibly wrong thing to do. On paper.

She took a breath, turned the knob on the bathroom door. Steam engulfed her, dancing on the mirror, shining up the tile floor. A giant gray towel waited on the counter. Mike was in there, beyond the smoked-glass shower doors.

She put the monitor on the counter, pulled off her cowl-neck top, pushed down her green cotton slacks. Opened the door and stepped in.

Mike turned around on a spin at the sudden burst of cool air. There was soap in his hair, water in his eyes. Mostly what she saw was somewhere around two hundred pounds of wet, naked man.

His first reaction was shock. That shocked silence lasted somewhere around a short millisecond. Initially his mind was clearly on something unrelated to sex. One look at her, and his body altered faster than a millisecond, too.

Before she'd taken a second step, he'd pulled her in and closed the glass door with the two of them inside. Before she could conceivably explain why she was here, he layered her against his hot, wet body and leveled a kiss on her.

If she'd just *known* she was going to do this crazy-fool thing, she'd have worn her black lace bra and matching panties, definitely not the pale yellow set from Target, on sale. She'd brushed her teeth. She just hadn't remembered the right clothes. She always remembered the right clothes for the occasion.

Only…well, it seemed the bra and thong were soaked in two seconds anyway. So was the rest of her. If she was going to drown in there, what possible difference could it make if she wasn't wearing her best bra?

And then the bra was gone. Tossed over the shower door.

Warm water splashed in her eyes, forcing her to close them…while Mike kept kissing her, swinging her against the warm, damp smooth wall, pinning her there. He held her hands flat against the tile, using his body to touch, to stroke, to incite. He groaned when his mouth left hers, only to trail a wreath of kisses down her throat.

He lifted her as if she weighed nothing, making it natural for her to wind her legs around his waist. When the nest between her legs rubbed against his belly, he swore. Then swore a second time when he nuzzled his cheeks between her breasts.

She recognized the tone in his voice. He was making that anger sound that she'd experienced earlier.

That vibrant anger. That infuriating, impatient, zesty anger.

Who knew he'd feel the same? Her heart opened in a shattering crack. She hadn't let anyone inside in forever. Hadn't trusted anyone, possibly ever, not this way. He'd been strung tight with denying what he needed, what he wanted. That ferocious hunger and yearning, to touch and be touched, was better denied than answered from the cold distance that came from failing marriages. Sex without trust had made her heart sore and scared.

But with Mike…it was right. The way it hadn't been right in a long time. He *liked* her. He valued her. It showed in his touch, his taste, his tenderness…his wildness.

He came up for a hoarse breath, asked, "Molly?"

She motioned outside the shower. "Brought monitor."

"Birth control?"

"What, you don't store condoms in the shower, waiting for me?"

He laughed, but it sounded a whole lot more like a groan. She rewarded him with a tiny bite from his ear. "I was giving up birth control, since I never planned to need it. Ever. Again. Until you. But for now I've got the long-term patch."

"Good."

That seemed to end the conversation. At least, he lost interesting in talking. So did she.

The damn man found the showerhead hose. She saw his sudden grin, saw his hand shoot up, grab the attachment by the showerhead. He eased her onto the tile floor, crossed her legs over his, and then played, pelting her throat, her tummy, her spine, between her legs...with warm, pulsing water.

Well, if *he* was in the mood to torture and tease... she was more than capable of stealing the hose and taking her turn. His laughter provoked another shattering crack in her heart. He was laughing with her. Sharing with her. It wasn't *using*.

It was giving.

And suddenly, as much fun—and teasing—as their playing had been, suddenly she wanted his hands. His skin. Him. Nothing between them.

His eyes darkened, sharpened. The water was still warm, blindingly warm, when he palmed her fanny, snuggled her closer, aimed inside. He slid in slowly, all slick slippery warmth, watching her reaction as he began a careful stroke...until he was all the way in. Slow turned into a canter, than a galloping hurry. She had a fearsome sensation of falling, a buildup of want so explosive, so consuming that she feared it would never end, never be over, never be appeased.

He whispered encouragement, praise, promise. When she peaked, her head fell back on a near scream...and he followed with an exultant groan as deep as hers.

She tried to breathe again, but couldn't. She stayed

wrapped around him like a scarf, her head in the crook of his shoulder, her body limp and wildly sated, not wanting to move…but the water started turning cool.

They both let out a yelp. He lifted his head. "I wondered when we'd run out of hot water. Darn it."

She was suddenly freezing. He was, too. He flipped off the faucets, helped her to her feet, and grabbed the thick gray towel to wrap around her. He had to step outside to find another. Towels were heaped in a basket on the floor; he took a black one for himself, but he wasn't concerned with drying himself off.

Instead, he rubbed her down until she was warm, kissing her brow, her neck, her shoulder en route. "I'm not afraid of much, Red. But I was afraid of this."

"Afraid of…?"

"Afraid that we'd be this good. I was hoping—if we did this—that it'd be kind of a clunker. Good, but not crazy good, so we could just get it out of our heads, go back to the friend thing, knowing the chemistry wasn't that bad of a problem."

She said, "For me. I'm afraid it's a mighty big problem."

For that, she got another kiss. On the nose. And a shine in his eyes that could have kindled fire. "You're not kidding. That was beyond anything I remember, Amanda. So now you've made our whole chemistry dilemma even worse."

"Hey. You were the one who dared me!"

His shaggy eyebrows arched. "Huh? You were the one doing all the daring. The way you walked. The way you looked at me. The way you smiled. The whole thing."

"I never did *anything*. It was you. Sending me those looks all the time."

"Hmm. So…is that what suddenly made you… come over here to climb in my shower out of the complete blue tonight?"

She looked at him, through wet hair and a smile that refused to stop coming. "No, Mike," she said softly. "I came over because…"

Startling both of them, Molly's voice suddenly crackled from the monitor on the counter. "Mom! Mommy! There's a lizard in the door! He's coming in here!"

Amanda sucked in a breath, but Mike was already shaking his head. "Don't worry about it for a minute. Of course you have to go. But I'd like to finish that conversation."

"Breakfast. My deck." But that was all she had time to say. Still wearing his towel, she plucked up her clothes, sprinted through his house and out the back door. Outside, it was darn near freezing on her bare feet and wet hair—but she ran like lightning, pelted into her own house.

"Mommy!"

She'd forgotten to bring the monitor back, but it

didn't matter. She could hear Molly's voice for herself now.

"I'm coming, honey!" She traded Mike's gray towel for a butterfly one from the downstairs bathroom, and scooted up the stairs. Out of breath, she paused in Molly's doorway. "I was taking a shower, honey. I need to put on a nightgown and I'll be right in."

"It's a horrible lizard. Purple and orange. With glasses. And pointy feet. *I'm* not afraid. But he was going to hurt you, Mommy. So I have to come sleep with you."

It wasn't how she hoped to end the evening, snuggled in a narrow twin bed with a four-year-old, Princess and Darling. Yet her daughter and the dog and kitten all slept as soundly as zombies.

She didn't. Her heart was still racing, her mind spinning, Mike's name humming in every beat of her pulse. Maybe she'd done the wrong thing. Maybe she'd done the right.

She was frighteningly unsure how this could possibly turn out well for both of them.

But she didn't regret what happened. Didn't, wouldn't, couldn't.

Amanda woke up in a tantalizingly high mood… until she glanced at the clock. Molly, Princess and Darling were already out and about somewhere, but the princess clock beside her daughter's bed claimed it was eight. Which meant she could have company from next door for breakfast before she'd had a chance to brush her teeth, much less to make anything to feed the four of them.

She flew out of bed, hurtled through drawers to find the appropriate dress-for-success attire—a frayed sweatshirt, old yoga pants. In the bathroom, she did the wash-face, brush-teeth thing, then swiped on two splashes of blush, braided her hair with a long scarf, loose, not tight, and didn't bother with shoes because there was no time. She hoped she looked like he usually did. Casual. Honest. Natural. Definitely not overly put together.

Molly, Princess and Darling all crowded her in the kitchen. She whipped up eggs, added a dab of cream cheese and cheddar, fresh chives…dropped a fork, then the spatula. Princess leaped on the counter in a cloud of white fur; both pets wanted to be fed and loved; Molly wanted a change in hairstyle *right now.* She started the toaster, pulled out the marmalade, poured OJ into a glass pitcher…chased outside to wipe down the glass table on the deck…chased back in to find Molly sampling the marmalade with a spoon.

Panic didn't set in. Not then. At least not totally. It was just that during all that frenzy of activity, a few teensy needling thoughts squeezed into her mind.

Such as…Mike had given her serious reasons why

he'd voted for the celibacy route. Her showing up in his shower wasn't exactly fair.

Such as…last night, it seemed terribly important that she not sit back, not be the kind of princess who needed a man to take charge. But by light of day, courage didn't look like courage anymore. It sort of looked brazen. It sort of looked like a pushy, brazen woman had shown up in his shower, specifically when he'd said he didn't want to be involved.

The more she thought…the more she wondered whether it was too late to hide under the nearest bed with heaps of blankets over her head.

She ran silverware and napkins and place settings out to the deck, ran back inside, cracked a nail on the door, shook it, turned the eggs, popped the first round of toast, heard the knock on the door.

Then panic set in.

"I know we're late," Mike said.

"That's okay, we're running just a tad late here, too." She smiled brilliantly, hoping he couldn't see that there was a gulp in her throat bigger than the state of Nevada.

He and Teddy were cleaned up, spiffed up. Teddy had a tucked-in shirt. Mike had a white polo that set off his tanned skin and a totally naked chin. He not only looked handsome beyond belief; he'd shaved. For her. And here she looked scruffier than his dog. He had to think she'd made no effort, where he so clearly had.

Their eyes met, and she almost dropped the eggs. Would have, if he hadn't swooped in and taken the bowl. "Let's help, guys," he told the kids, which was an outstanding idea.

He not only looked jumpable; the look of him brought on more nerves, because she was afraid she would. Jump him. At the earliest opportunity. Apparently now that the Brazen Gene had been let out of her closet, it was going to be tough locking it back in.

Mike and the kids carted everything outside. She brought up the rear with the OJ pitcher and glasses— which Mike took out of her hands before she could drop them. The morning still had a sting of a chill, but the grass was diamond-studded with dew, the sun soaking-bright.

The kids dove in as if no one had ever fed them… but that didn't last long. They started making faces at each other. Molly, ever the lady, exposed a mouthful of scrambled eggs. Teddy pulled his eyes apart with his fingers. Both of them pulled out their lips.

"It's hard to believe they're going to be part of civilized society in another twenty years, isn't it?" she asked Mike.

He laughed. Not a loud laugh. But a throaty, sexy laugh. Turned her on all over again. "You promise it'll only take twenty years?"

A forkful of egg arced in the air, landed in the

lilies. "Hey, guys. That's over the top. Who did it?" Amanda demanded.

"Not me," Molly said.

"Not me," Teddy said.

She pretended to buy into that bologna, turning a stern expression on Mike. "Mr. Mike, if you throw food again, you're going to get a time-out, and I'm not kidding."

That set the kids to giggling again. It was a lot easier, entertaining the four-year-olds than facing Mike alone. But eventually they got too squirmy to sit still, and Amanda gave them permission to go inside and play a game.

Unfortunately, once the kids deserted ship, the insanely messy table was the only thing between her and Mike. She'd felt his eyes on her, his smile on her, all through the picnic breakfast…but it was the first time she could really look back at him. At least in that naked way. That raw-nerves honest way.

"Did you sleep okay?" he asked her.

"Slept good. Just not long enough. You?"

"Like a log. Although I wish you hadn't had to run home. Was Molly all right?"

"Yes. It was just her lizard nightmare. But I still needed to be there."

"Of course you did."

Conversation stalled like a dead battery. Mike's eyes never left hers. Finally he put his elbows on the table, hunching forward. "My guess is the kids'll interrupt us in two minutes or less. So either we dive into talking about last night. Or let it be. You have a vote?"

"Better talk."

"Ok. The last thing I expected was a naked woman in my shower last night. Was there maybe something that triggered that happening? That I should know about?"

"Well…" How could she explain something that just all clicked in her head all at once? "It was because of Molly. In the fight yesterday with the second-grader."

Mike frowned. "I saw the shiner. But somehow it's hard for me to imagine how the two issues could be connected."

"Because. When I was talking to Molly—about fighting and violence never being a good answer—she got her back up. Some days she is *such* a red-head. And even though I'm not condoning her hitting anyone…later, it just kept occurring to me. Molly's viewpoint was right. Sometimes it's the girl who has to take charge."

"Amanda. Try to concentrate. Because I'm getting more lost instead of less."

Why did she have to be such an incoherent mess this morning? When it mattered? When everybody told her she was articulate in a crisis, how come she had such a hard time with Mike?

She clasped her hands together. "This is the thing.

We've had this…connection between us. Neither of us want our kids hurt. Neither of us want it to go too far. But I just kept thinking, Mike, we're *friends*. We're both smart. I think there's a level where we trust each other. So why couldn't we do something we both want—and maybe need—as long as we're both careful? But then…I thought…you really couldn't be the one to take the plunge."

"And why would that be?"

"For the same reason my daughter hit that little girl. And your son didn't. Because you're raising your son to be a gentleman. The same way you are."

Something cooled in his eyes. A ruler stiffened his spine. "Trust me, Amanda. I'm not."

"You are. In every way." Her voice was warm, sincere…but from his expression, she seemed to be hitting him totally the wrong way.

"So." His voice turned softer than butter. "*You* made the first move, because you didn't think I had the guts to?"

"No. Good grief, Mike. No. That wasn't what I meant at all—"

"I think it's pretty clear. You and Molly think we're the kind of guys who can't do our own fighting."

Now she was getting confused—as well as palm-cold anxious. "This wasn't about fighting. Neither of us want our kids to fight. Both of us are teaching our kids that violence is not a way to solve anything—"

"I'm not talking about the kids. I'm talking about

us. And if the only reason you showed up last night is because you didn't think I'd ever find the guts to—"

"Wait. Just wait. That's not what—"

Teddy and Molly barreled out of the house at the same time, shrieking and laughing...and soaking wet.

Amanda couldn't remember what they said they were going to play—fish? Candy Land? A marble game? So she wasn't sure which culprit had unearthed the squirt guns from the closet in the back room. Of course, it didn't matter who.

She shot an unhappy look at Mike—who didn't look back. He grabbed his kid. She grabbed hers.

There wasn't going to be any more private talking. Not now. Amanda felt a sinking sense of loss. She told herself that you couldn't lose what you never had.

But Mike's expression had become starched, his posture rigid.

She'd hurt him. Really hurt him.

She'd bumbled a moment that seriously mattered—and she had no idea how to make it right.

Chapter Ten

A half hour later, Teddy didn't object to a ride in the truck, but he kept sneaking peeks at him. "Dad. Molly and I didn't break anything or hurt anything. We just got wet."

"I know."

"But you look so mad."

"I'm not mad."

"Then how come you keep looking mad, if you're not mad?"

Mike declenched his jaw, rolled the iron out of his shoulders, smiled at his son. "I think you and I have earned a big day off."

"I think so, too!" Teddy agreed, and then added, "What does 'a day off' mean?"

"It means you and I are going to have a guy day. We're going fishing. In a lake. In a boat. Where there are no phones and no doorbells and no one can reach us. You like that idea?"

"I love it! I love fishes! I've always loved fishes!"

The whole afternoon, Mike tried to get his head back on track. There were tons of places to snag a rental boat, buy some live bait, set Teddy up with a fun afternoon. The sun was blazing, the lake silvery-calm, the sky a pure blue canvas without a single cloud. Teddy caught a little bass that fought like the devil, then a bigger one, a catfish, one pretty pike.

The whole time, Mike felt lower than a skunk, although he did his damnedest to hide the clunky mood from his son.

But he was hurting.

From the day he'd met Amanda, he warned himself not to fall for her.

She was the wrong woman—the most contrary redhead he'd ever come across. And it was the wrong time—for all the reasons they both knew and had commiserated about.

But last night, when she'd shown up in his shower... he'd known.

He hadn't just fallen. He'd leaped straight off the cliff, so deep, so hard, there was no climbing back. She'd scraped past layers no one else ever had. She'd *touched* him...because she'd taken that kind of huge emotional risk. With him. For him. And for all their play, he'd tried to lavish her with tenderness and care and skill. The best of who he was as a lover.

So when she'd pulled the "friends" on him this morning, it ripped. But the details—that she thought she'd had to seduce him—as if he weren't man enough to do the seducing…it just sent him into a crash funk.

He'd been *trying* to play by her rules by not touching her. He'd been *trying* to be a decent guy, for once.

Amanda was nothing like his ex, Mike knew, but suddenly it felt like new song, old refrain. Amanda was the cultured, classy type. She thought he was fine for a roll in the hay—but not good enough to fit in with her image of a long-term mate.

Teddy snoozed the whole way home, and Mike had the quiet sunset drive to put it all in perspective. That's it. He'd shut up from here on. Go back to the rules they'd agreed on to begin with.

He'd be a *friend*.

Nothing else.

His resolve lasted a whole four days. When the phone rang, he had thick gloves on and was working in the basement with Teddy's worm farm—knee-deep in a project that didn't smell good, didn't look good and needed to be done.

He'd have let the machine pick up—Teddy was with him, and there was no other emergency that couldn't wait five minutes that he could imagine. But when the machine clicked on, he heard Amanda's voice.

"Mike? I'm pretty sure you're there. You probably just can't come to the phone. But...I had a problem come up, and I was hoping—"

That's all that went down before he'd taken the stairs three at a time and grabbed the landline in the kitchen. "I'm here. I was just downstairs. What's up?"

He knew from the way she said his name, from everything in her voice, that she was stressed and strung tight.

"I hate to ask you. But I have to be in court at one. I didn't ask my parents to babysit, because frankly, I'd rather they didn't know until afterward. They get all upset, and this was something I didn't want spilling on Molly inadvertently. Anyway, I called an agency. They sent over a babysitter with fabulous credentials. She got here at 11:00 a.m. I kicked her out three minutes ago. There was just no way—"

"You need me to watch Molly."

There. He heard her take a breath. *Breathe.* "Yes. If you could. It's too late for me to set up anything else. I have to be in the car before 11:30 a.m. And—"

"Hey. Molly'll be fine with me. You know that. Don't even think twice."

The girls arrived five minutes later. Amanda was dressed like he'd never seen her, wearing judge-sober navy, nothing like her usual put-together thing. Just a navy skirt, white blouse, all tidy and meticulous, makeup on the spare. Her hair was rolled up in some kind of coil in back; God knew how she'd tamed it, but it was pinned and straight within an inch of its life. She had a smile on. He didn't know whose smile it was, but it sure as hell wasn't Amanda's.

"Thanks, Mike," was all she said.

"You need someone to go with you?" He couldn't take his eyes off her strained face.

"No. Everything's fine. I just needed help with Molly—" she shot a reassuring smile at her daughter "—because she would have been completly bored all afternoon, stuck sitting in a chair while I was at this little meeting."

It wasn't a little meeting, but Mike got it. That was the story for Molly.

"Hey, she'll have a good time with us. Right, Mol? And don't worry about the time. We'll be here."

She took a breath, thanked him again, gave him a house key in case he needed anything for Molly... then bent down to kiss her daughter and she was off.

He turned to Molly. It appeared to be a Cat Day. She wore a top with pastel cats, carried two stuffed cats and had a purse the size of a half dollar that looked like a cat. There were two jelly beans inside the purse. She gave one to Teddy right off, so she could have the other, but so far she wasn't talking to him.

He hunkered more to her height. "Here's the deal. We're not doing something you're likely to have fun with, right this minute. We're bringing the worm farm up from the basement, because they're ready to live outside in the shed. And there are enough worms to start feeding the frogs in the water garden. But that's all pretty dirty work. Nothing you'd probably like."

She nodded.

"But you could sit on the table in the yard and just watch us for a bit, okay? We'll get this done as soon as we can. And after that, Teddy and I'll get cleaned up. And then we could all go for an ice cream cone. Or to the library. Or watch a movie. Or go to the park. Or…"

"Go shopping," Molly supplied.

That hadn't been on his list, would never have been on his list, but he nodded. "That's just what I was hoping you might like to do."

"I really don't want to do anything. My mom did *not* want to go to this meeting. Something is *wrong* and I don't like it. But I guess I could sit here for a while." She perched on the deck table, crossed her legs like her mother and motioned like a princess for the boys to proceed.

Mike hesitated, thinking maybe he should get her to talk if she was upset. But without knowing what Amanda was dealing with exactly, he figured he'd better try a wait-see before trying to dive into Molly's little head. As it happened, he didn't have to worry about either choice, because she'd ambled down to the water garden, holding one of her stuffed cats, before two minutes had passed.

"Mr. Mike, your stones are all wrong."

He'd framed the kidney-shaped water garden with stones, both to keep down the liner and to make the project look "done." "What's wrong with them?"

"You just didn't put them in a pretty way. They don't look right."

He looked at his brilliantly designed minipond, then raised an eyebrow at the pint-size diva. "So how do you think they should look?"

She showed him, and damned if she wasn't right. After she'd rearranged all the stupid stones, the whole setup looked better landscaped.

"You're pretty smart," he told her.

"That's what my mom says. But grown-ups never listen to me. I don't know why." She was ignoring Teddy as if he didn't exist, but that was possibly because his son had his hands full of worms and was dying to get her attention. "Only, now you need some lights."

"What kind of lights?"

"You know. The kind of little lights that you put outside. They don't have cords. They have to get sun during the day to make them work. Then they'd make your pond look pretty at night." She frowned.

"I think you need four." She motioned where she wanted them.

She *was* a miniature of her mother. "I think you're right again."

"I could give you more ideas, if you want." Once she opened up, of course, she couldn't shut up. She supervised lunch, which included how to properly wash hands, how Mike should cut the bread crusts and how napkins were folded. Once they all sat down—including Slugger and Cat—she opened up about Amanda.

"I've been thinking about it," she said, "and I think I know where my mom is. It's all about heat."

"Heat," Mike echoed.

"Yup. Heat. I'll bet her meeting is with the vet. Because when we took Darling to the vet a while ago—the new vet, the one we're going to now—he said it might be too late. And then my mom sent me out to the waiting room. And when we got home, that's when we had to start locking Darling up in the laundry room. Or she had to wear a diaper when she was walking around. It's all about in heat."

"I see."

"Darling doesn't have to wear a diaper anymore. So I thought everything was okay. But then Mom had to go to this meeting. And that's the only thing I know she was worried about."

Okay, he just couldn't completely let that go. "You know what? Your mom may be worried about something, just like you're thinking. But you might want to remember, she's really strong and smart."

"Yeah, she is," Molly agreed.

"Being smart doesn't mean you'll never have a problem. Everybody has problems. But I think you can stop worrying about your mom. She's so strong and smart, that I'm positive she'll find a way to work it out."

"I sort of know that." Molly sighed. "I just don't like it when she doesn't tell me everything."

Teddy, clearly tired of being cut out, interrupted to say, "If you get to talk to my dad, then I get to talk to your mom."

"Yeah. So?"

"And if you get to come over here, then I should get to go over to your house sometimes."

"Sure," Molly said.

"And I worry about my dad, too. All the time."

"Yeah? What about?"

Teddy had to think. "Just things. Like when my mom isn't nice to him. Things like that."

The kids had a competitive argument over who was the best kid/who worried most/who took best care of their mom or dad. Mike felt like a humorous fly on the wall; they battled back and forth as if he weren't even there. The afternoon filled up. He took the kids for ice cream, then had to find a potty. A trip to Target thankfully solved Molly's shopping need, where he bought exactly the lights she told him to—that required another potty break. By three o'clock in the afternoon, he brought out cards on the deck and played fish forever. At least twenty minutes.

About then he started glancing at his watch. It might be too soon to start watching for Amanda, but he figured whatever had gone right—or wrong—about the custody hearing had already happened. She was either hugely relieved...or hugely upset.

His mother called. She wanted them over for dinner on Sunday. The phone rang again. It was a headhunter who specialized in attorney positions and wanted Mike as a client. The kids settled on the rug with the dog in front of a Disney flick.

Mike told himself to get the mail, get some bills paid, use the quiet time to tackle some chores.

But it was four-thirty by then, and Amanda still wasn't home.

He knew how courts worked. How custody hearings went. Amanda had no way of knowing how long she'd be gone, and she'd have called him if she expected to be crazy late, or if anything had happened. She'd never have left her daughter hanging.

So there was no reason for him to worry.

And he wasn't worried exactly.

He was just glued to the window.

At ten to five, her white SUV zoomed into the driveway. The sound of the car sent Slugger baying and Cat snarling at the dog door to confront the arrival. Molly and Teddy didn't budge—they were near the end of the movie—but when Mike said, "Your mom's just pulling in, Mol," the little one bounced to her feet.

Slugger and Cat beat everyone else out the door to greet her, then came kids, with Mike bringing up the rear. By the time he got a look, she was bending down to give Molly a giant hug and kiss, so he couldn't see her face.

Teddy got in there, to start explaining that he thought he should have time at her house, too, and Amanda was agreeing with him. "I was thinking of something we could do that would be fun for you. You like getting your hands dirty, don't you?"

"Yeah, I do," Teddy confirmed.

"In fact, Teddy, I was thinking…maybe you could come over when we have a baking afternoon. Lots of flour all over the place. Lots of messes. Lots of squishing butter between your fingers. We could make pies or cookies or something. That sound okay to you?"

"That sounds like something I've wanted to do my whole life. And nobody ever let me before."

After Teddy's turn, his hound had to be petted, and Molly was still talking to her mom nonstop…but finally, finally, she lifted her head. "Hey, neighbor. Did you survive?"

"We had a blast."

"Uh-huh. What do I owe you? A day in a padded

cell? Brownies? Cookies for the rest of your life? Slave labor cleaning floors? Pizza?"

She made the kids laugh…he did, too. "Let me think on it."

"Yeah, you probably need a five-hour nap, huh?"

He chuckled again at her teasing, since she clearly wanted him to. "Everything go okay for you?"

"Sure did," she said heartily. "Tell you about it when I get a chance. In the meantime…I'd better get Molly in and my brood fed and watered. Thanks, Mike. I really, really appreciate it."

"Hey, no sweat. Anytime," he said, and meant it. She looked at him, her expressions, her words, as if he were seriously a cherished friend, sincerity radiating from her tone and smile.

They were doing the friend thing really well, he thought.

And wished he could kick a mountain in the shins.

Something had whipped the hell out of her in that custody hearing. He didn't know who won what—or who lost what—but Amanda's eyes had the fierce brightness of a lioness. She was hurting. Bad.

Mike felt a sudden, sharp ripping sensation. Her hurting wasn't supposed to be his business.

She didn't want a hero. She wanted a friend. She didn't want someone to beat up her enemies, to protect her, to watch over her.

She wanted a friend. She didn't want him in the

YOURS, MINE & OURS

parts of her life that involved pain or fear or any of
that other rotten life crap. She just wanted a friend.

Those were her rules.

Well, they'd played it her way. Now they were
going to play it his way.

Chapter Eleven

Well, Amanda thought, she'd handled that reasonably well. Or as well as she possibly could have. Mike hadn't guessed she was upset. Neither of the kids sensed anything was wrong…although Molly was still sneaking questions at bedtime.

"I think you're going to be a prosecuting attorney when you grow up," Amanda said as she snuggled Molly in fresh sheets and her favorite doll of the week.

"I don't know what a prosecutor attorney is."

"It means someone who's really good at asking questions. And at finding ways to get the answers they want." She bent over to kiss Molly good-night. "Did you have a good time next door?"

"I told you that already. I had a great time. I didn't scream about the worms. I just ignored Teddy when he was being awful that way. And I helped Mr. Mike in a whole lot of ways."

"You did, huh?"

"He thinks I'm smart."

"Everybody thinks you're smart. Because you are."

"I know. But he *listens* to me. Like I wasn't a little kid. Like I was somebody you want to listen to."

"Well, that's really good." The fairy night-light stayed on, but Amanda switched off the pink lamp with the fringe shade

"Mommy. Don't go. I need some mommy time."

"We can have all the mommy time you want tomorrow. But it's late tonight."

"Just a couple more minutes!"

Amanda wasn't positive she could hold it together for a "couple more minutes," but she sank back on the bed and said, "Okay, whiffer-sniffer."

Molly giggled. "Thank you very much, Bonkle-wonkle." It was an old game, always worth some smiles, but then Molly got more serious. "I don't know what a meeting is. But I don't like it, when I don't know where you are."

"A meeting is just a word to describe when people are getting together for some reason. And you may not always know where I am, Mol, but you will always, always be able to reach me. No matter where I am or what I'm doing, I'll always have the cell phone on for you."

"But something could happen to the cell phone. It could break. Or fall in the sink. Or drop in a lake. Or a car could run over it."

"You're right. Even having a very, very, very good cell phone isn't totally foolproof. Things happen. But I would never leave you with anyone who couldn't find another way to reach me."

"Okay. I think. Mom."

"What?"

"You were at the vet today, weren't you?"

"No. Where'd you get that idea?"

"It just came into my mind. I don't know how it got there. But if you weren't at the vet's, where were you?"

Amanda had prepared that answer before coming home, so it could slip off her tongue, fast and easy. "I was talking with some attorneys about some business."

"Well, don't talk to those attorneys again. Just talk to Mr. Mike. He's an attorney. We don't need any other attorneys. And then you wouldn't have to be gone for a whole afternoon."

"Hey. I've been gone lots of afternoons, and you never had a sweat before. Think of swimming with Grandma. And the Curious Kids Museum with Grandma and Grandpa. And you used to do morn-

ings in daycare when I was working. You know I
always come back."

"I know."

"I can't be with you every second. And you can't
be with me every second. But that's okay. Then we
come back together and can tell each other about our
adventures. Right?"

"Yeah. Right."

"So are we square?"

"We are very, very, very square. But, Mom."

"What, hon?"

"Just don't go wherever you went today, okay? Anywhere else is okay. But not to that *meeting* again."

"I'll try my best, ragamuffin. And now, you try
your best to sleep really good, okay?"

"One more kiss?"

"Three more kisses, and don't you dare try to escape a great big old hug, too."

There. A few more giggles, more hugs, and finally,
Amanda could ease the door closed and tiptoe out
into the hall.

Her smile died; her shoulders sagged, and she
lifted a shaky hand to pull the pins out of her hair.
Her mother had left a message on the machine. An
old friend from high school had left another message,
said he'd be in town over the weekend, and hoped
they could get together.

She turned the volume off the phone, switched
off the light in the kitchen. She wanted a shower, to

shake off the dirt of this terrible day. She wanted a glass of something alcoholic, too, but couldn't work up enough ambition to actually get it.

Feeling boneless-tired, she sank into the blue chair in the living room and leaned forward with her head in her hands.

Most women she knew felt destroyed by a divorce. Maybe she'd been there, too, but she'd tried to see it as an opportunity to build herself into a better woman. A stronger woman. The kind of competent woman who wouldn't just *let* bad things happen to her because she wasn't strong enough to face the facts.

Well. She'd faced some facts this afternoon.

She'd failed to protect her daughter.

The only job in the universe that mattered.

She felt a claw on her ankle, sighed, and lifted Darling to her lap. A heap of purring fur leaped to the top of the chair and then delicately tried to wind herself like a scarf around Amanda's neck. She loved both pets. Hugely. And they were overdue attention today, but just then, all she wanted was some nice, long, wallowing silence.

Somehow, someway, she had to get up the next morning.

Somehow, someway, she had to find a way to say the right maternal things to Molly.

Somehow, someway, she had to find a way to believe she hadn't failed in everything that mattered to her.

"Hey. I knocked. But I wasn't sure if you heard me...and the back door wasn't locked..."

Her head shot up. The last person she expected to see was Mike, much less standing in the arch of her kitchen, holding a two-inch kitty-cat purse. The purse looked downright funny, hanging from the beefy wrist of a six-foot-two hunk.

More to the point, she'd assumed he'd be comatose by now, after dealing with two four-year-olds for most of the day. For sure he was wearing torn old jeans and a tee that looked as if it lost a wrestling match—it was that wrinkled and ragged. But he wasn't.

He looked like the Mike she'd fallen in love with. Brash and unbrushed, a smile as natural as sunshine, that easy, earthy way of moving that was so purely male. It wasn't hard to imagine him fighting down and dirty. It was easy to imagine him cleaned up, in a navy suit and white shirt, fighting to win with a force-ful presence, and slow, quiet words. It was just as easy to imagine him being there, through thick and thin, no minor irritation like earthquakes or avalanches keeping him from those he loved.

He was just a bigger-than-life kind of guy. It wasn't his fault.

But she wasn't going to be on the list of loved ones he dug through those avalanches for. As often as she remembered the night they made love, she winced every time her heart replayed the messy hurts that showed up the next day.

And faster than pride, she straightened. Possibly she couldn't find another fake smile today to save her life, but she tried for a normal, pleasant expression. "Aw, Mike, I'm sorry you went to the trouble. You didn't have to bring over Molly's purse. We'd have gotten it tomorrow."

"Yeah, right. I've spent one-on-one time with Molly now. Once she realized she'd forgotten something as important as this—" he carefully removed the purse from his wrist and set it on the couch "—I figured there'd be hell to pay for someone. I didn't want it to be me."

She still couldn't smile, but darn it, almost. "Uh-oh. Am I sensing she was a tad difficult this afternoon?"

"Are you kidding? She was perfect. I'm in love with her. She is absolutely honest. Just says everything like it is. That was cool," he said, as if they were starting another conversation, "about the two jelly beans in the purse."

"What? Oh. Yes. I told her, one for Teddy, one for her. I figured they'd be a conversation breaker when she first came over—"

"Great thinking, Mom. It really worked. And in the meantime…" From behind his back, he produced a sturdy box with fancy lettering. "I had something to celebrate. Had a bottle of Talisker hidden away for the past couple of years, needed an excuse to bring it out. Share a glass with me?"

"Thanks, Mike, but no. Honestly, I'm half asleep. Just really, really tired—"

"Just one short glass."

"I'd like to, really, but just not tonight—"

It was like talking to a brick wall. Maybe he didn't hear her, because he went into her kitchen and returned with two glasses. And maybe he couldn't see her shaking her head.

"Very short. I promise," he said genially, not looking at her face, just gathering the box, the glasses, some paper towels for napkins, and then settling—not on the couch or other chairs—but on the ottoman right in front of her. "You hold the glasses, okay? It'll take me a minute to get this open."

It was going to take him longer, because Darling leaped off Amanda's lap and headed for Molly's room. Princess, on the other hand, decided she'd rather sit on Mike's lap than hers.

She loved them. But just then she wasn't up for the cuteness of pets, or Mike this close, or Mike here at all. She'd put on a strong face all day. For Molly, she could do that. But for Mike…she wasn't sure she could fake anything with Mike.

He didn't act as if he noticed anything wrong. Just kept talking. "This cat has more fur than a coat. And I thought she was a kitten. You're turning into a little white pumpkin, aren't you…? Teddy's at my parents'. His first overnight. It's a big deal. He's been afraid to be away from me at night ever since the divorce. Had nightmares when we've tried it. But…out of the blue, he said he wanted to, so I called them up…and they both leaped at the idea. I'll be glued to a cell phone all night, but hoping it'll work out okay."

"Is that what you wanted to celebrate?"

"No, not that. I'm up for celebrating that another time—assuming he makes it all night without my being called to come get him. Okay, here you go…" He'd opened the blue box, produced the bottle and opened it, all without making the purring machine on his lap even budge. He poured equal amounts in two glasses, just filling them halfway, and handed her one, but with a caution.

"Now, this isn't a drinking drink. It's a sipping drink. A slow-sip-and-savor drink. The only place this is made is on the Isle of Skye. Aged ten years plus. And there's no talking or discussion when you take your first slow sip. You just close your eyes and let it happen."

He wasn't talking fast; he just kept on talking in that slow, easy way of his. She couldn't get a word in, much less an objection. She gave up, accepted the glass, and just figured she'd finish the drink quickly and *then* coax him to go home.

"Wait, wait, wait!"

She lowered the glass at his admonition, saw his grin.

"You don't drink this without a toast." He lifted

his glass to hers, clinked. "To parents of four-year-olds."

"Good one." Again she lifted the glass, but before it reached her lips, the scent hit her nose. "Hold on. What is this?"

"Scotland's most famous single malt."

"You mean, whiskey?"

He shot her a glower. "When you speak of Talisker, you speak in reverent tone and terms. It's Scotch whiskey. You've never had it?"

"Actually, no. I'm usually a wine girl. Not that I haven't had a mint julep or Manhattan at a party sometimes, but—"

"Okay. Another toast." He clinked her glass again. "To virgin Talisker tasters."

"Mike. You're acting awfully goofy tonight."

"Uh-huh. Taste."

She took a slow, careful sip. Initially the liquid felt soft and smooth on her tongue, interesting, different… but that was before the fire. Flames shot internally straight to the top of her brain. Smoke whooshed out her nose, throat and possibly her ears. Embers drizzled down her esophagus. Tears welled in her eyes. Her entire living room blurred, tilted sideways.

Eventually the smoke cleared. The pale blue chairs and blueberry-blue carpet stopped moving. The soft light from the purple-and-blue Tiffany lamp looked normal again. Mike was hunched over the ottoman, less than two feet from her face, his exultant grin just full of the devil. "I knew you'd love it."

"Love?" She opened her mouth, released some more fumes. "To tell you the truth…" She glanced at the amber liquid, considered, and couldn't think of a single reason why she needed to tell the truth. He obviously loved the drink. "I think this may possibly be the best thing that's happened to me all day."

"Atta girl. Another toast. This one to redheads. But *only* to redheads who happened to be named Molly or Amanda."

"Okay. Listen. I love the goofball thing. But, Mike. I'm not a big drinker, and I don't do hangovers, and—"

"Me, either. That stopped being fun before I was nineteen. We're not drinking a lot—I promise. Talisker is only for special occasions. You never level it. At most—no matter how much you beg—you can only have two glasses, max."

She frowned, studying him, unsure where all his high spirits and energy and foolishness were coming from. It wasn't as if she wanted to burst his bubble. If he had good news to share…well, that's what being a friend was about, wasn't it?

And especially after this afternoon, she knew she could never be more—no matter what she felt for Mike, or what she'd hoped for.

So she lifted her glass—tapped his—and said, "My turn to make a toast."

* * *

Talk about a slow drinker. It took her a full half hour just to sip through a shot, and probably the same amount of time to level a second.

Mike never wanted her inebriated. He just wanted her to talk. She was wound so tight, he was wary that she could crack into a zillion pieces.

And even after two shots, he figured the bottom line. No amount of liquor was going to loosen her up. But maybe from exhaustion, or the late hour, she curled her bare legs under her and kind of hovered inside the pale blue wing chair.

"You told me before this that your ex was applying for partial custody. So this was it? That hearing?" By the time he got around to asking, he tried to make his voice as lazy and safe as a hum in the night.

"Yup." She didn't seem to want to continue, but finally, out it came. "Thom won. I lost."

"Tell me."

"It's a real short story. I failed her. There's only one darned thing in this life that I *have* to do right—and that's protect Molly. And I failed big-time."

Mike unclenched his jaw. Maybe later he'd find out Thom's address and tar and feather the son of a seadog. But just then he was listening. And he was going to stay calm while listening if it killed him. "There has to be a little more to it."

"Thom was pushing for joint custody. Obviously I've known that for a while. And here's the thing. He's her father. I never wanted to deny him the right to be her father, or to spend time with her. She needs her father and loves him. But damn it, Mike…"

"Keep talking."

"It isn't about being a dad for him. It's about manipulation. Because when she's over there, he's somehow an absentee. There'll be some woman friend of his that does the babysitting. He doesn't actually *want* joint custody, because he doesn't spend half the time with her that he could. He just wants not to have to pay me child support."

"Keep talking."

And about then, she bolted out of the blue wing chair, as if sitting still even a second longer was impossible. She was still wearing the navy-and-white outfit thing she'd put together for the court, but it was coming undone mighty fast now. The white shirt was no longer tucked in, no longer buttoned at the neck. She'd lost the shoes. The navy skirt was twisted around. Her hands started gesturing. The hair got wilder. She stumbled and circled and ambled around in her bare feet, not crying. Sometimes her eyes spit out some moisture, but those tears were hot and mad, not soft.

"I don't *need* the child support. But I've been using that money to put together a college fund for Mol. He makes over six figures. Don't you think it's fair that he contribute?"

"Absolutely," Mike agreed.

"I told the judge that Thom cancels half the time he sets up a visitation with Molly. I told him that he's repeatedly left her with strange women she doesn't know, and that often enough she comes back upset and shaken up. The judge didn't care."

"Who's the judge?" Mike asked, thinking there was another tar-and-feather candidate. He knew a good number of judges, but not so many in the family court setup. She told him the name. Unfortunately all he knew about the guy was that he'd been on the bench for over a decade.

"The judge said…that unless there's abuse or specific proof of neglect, that Thom is entitled to more time. Initially he didn't grant equal custody. But as of right now, Thom gets an overnight every two weeks. *Mike.* I'm supposed to just spring this on Molly. After she just talked to me about not wanting to spend nights there!"

She spun around, and he saw her expression in the colored light from the Tiffany lamp. "Aw, Red. That's the worst sting, isn't it?"

"It is. This is supposed to start this coming weekend, which means I have to start talking to her about tomorrow. My job as a mom is—obviously—to make this as smooth and stress-free as I can. So I have to say something like, 'Hey, lovebug, you know your dad loves you, and you'll have fun on those sleepovers, and you know I'll be there when you get back.' So I'll *try.* But, Mike, I'm afraid it'll come out fake, because it's such a lie. She doesn't have a choice. How am I supposed to make her do something that I think is wrong? And make out like I think it's okay?"

"I hear you."

"When I got out the courtroom…Thom grabbed my hand. He said there'd be another custody hearing after this. I could count on it. And in the next one, he'd win full joint custody. That I shouldn't kid myself. He'll end up not paying a dime of child support."

"Come here."

"It's not *about* the money. It's about his using Molly in the wrong way."

"Come here."

"It's about her feeling she's lied to when she's with him. That's why she doesn't feel safe there. And I always promised her that I'd protect her. And now I can't."

"Come here."

She heard him, because she finally quit pacing around like a caged cat and faced him. "Mike, you can't help me. And if you could, I wouldn't want you to. I need to fight my own battles. And I swear, I'm *trying*. This is just the worst kind of thing to lose. I feel cut off at the knees. I failed my daughter."

That was it. Mike strode over, scooped an arm under her legs, and lifted her in his arms.

He'd wanted her to talk. Well, she had. She'd spilled thoroughly. Only, now she was saying such ridiculous things that she obviously wasn't in a reasonable mood.

And no one, but no one, could be more unreasonable than Red when she was upset.

Come to think of it…he was damned good at being unreasonable when he was upset, too. And right now, he was more than upset.

For her.

And with her.

Chapter Twelve

Amanda was beyond shocked. She had no idea what triggered Mike, much less what changed him from a listening, empathetic friend into a wildly out-of-control lover. She couldn't think. She couldn't breathe.

She *really* couldn't breathe. Once she'd started talking about the afternoon in court, the story had burst out like a runaway freight train. She hadn't cried, but her throat was thick with unshed tears... and Mike, out of nowhere, took her mouth in a deep kiss.

He'd picked her up as if she were lighter than pearls and just...taken off. He seemed to be careening up the stairs to her bedroom, because the pale lamplight in the living room had disappeared and they were galloping somewhere in the darkness. His shoulder bumped into a wall.

That didn't stop him from kissing her.

Nothing seemed to stop him from kissing her.

She was a disaster. Surely he'd noticed? She was unbrushed, undone, un-everything. She felt sick, anxious, lost. Her self-worth index seemed to be hovering around a negative ten.

And still he kissed her. He lifted his head for a gulp of air, smiled at her as if they both had something to smile about, then dipped down again. The last time he'd seen her bedroom, she—and the room— had been covered with paint. Moonlight streamed through the froth of curtains, ribbonlike on the thick, soft carpeting she'd put in.

The next time he came up for air, he dragged his T-shirt over his head, then started stripping her. He didn't seem to notice that she had drastically low self-esteem issues. He seemed to esteem every part of her quite thoroughly. He pulled down the zipper on her navy town skirt...popped off the button on her proper white blouse.

She should have smacked him from here to Timbuktu.

She considered it.

Temporarily, she seemed to be kissing him back and fumbling for the snap on his jeans...but she was still considering it.

He groaned as if she were killing him...when he was the one being the devil. He backed her to the bed edge, slipped her bra straps down, then laid her down on the poufy, soft comforter. The comforter didn't last long. He pushed away the covers and the pillows in one long swoop...then swooped back on her.

"You prepared to suffer?" he asked her.

The question made as much sense as anything else he'd done, but it wasn't like he gave her time to answer. His face dipped in and out of moonlight, and he made her giddy, the way he looked at her. As if it was his first time with a woman, and he'd waited a hundred years—not just for this—but for *her*.

That tongue of his. His hands. He made it seem like no woman ever had more gorgeous knees. More delectable elbows. More fascinating navels. It didn't seem to occur to him that these weren't erogenous zones. You couldn't seduce a woman by kissing her elbow.

Except her.

He seemed to be seducing her, no matter what he touched, no matter where, no matter how. She wasn't sure how a woman who could have been so, so low earlier in the evening could somehow, someway, now feel more powerful than any woman alive.

He seemed to be the somehow and someway.

He played and kept playing, until her skin had a silken sheen, and her heart was thundering a symphonic drum and she couldn't stop touching him back.

She felt on fire, inside and out, with need, with want, with…love.

"Enough," she said.

"I haven't even gotten started."

With the sudden superwoman power she'd developed, she twisted and miraculously moved him around until she was on top of him, and he was lying at her mercy on the rumpled sheets. "I've had it with you, Mike."

"I'm sorry."

"Oh, no. You're not sorry. But you will be."

"Hey. Red?"

"No more talking."

"I just wanted to mention. I'm in love with you. I don't know if it's right or wrong, sane or insane. This isn't going away. It's *bad*. The worse case I've ever had. Times a hundred. I thought I knew what love was. Until you."

"If you think that's going to get you out of trouble, think again," she said. Being a man, he probably wanted to go fast. Tough.

She sipped in a sigh as she closed around him, feeling how he filled her, how they connected, perfect as a lock and key. She was the lock.

He was the key.

No one else had ever brought out the redhead in her. She'd always been laced up. Liked being laced up. Except with Mike. She had a terrible feeling it would always be that way with him. That she wouldn't be able to hold back. That he'd bring out the lusty and earthy side of her, even when she had always, always liked everything tidy.

She lifted, sank…testing a rhythm, then finding one that seemed as natural as flying. "I love you right back," she whispered, and then couldn't talk anymore. Her heart took off in a soar, past earth, past sky, into a place where she felt weak with yearning, fierce with wanting. On fire, with need, for him, with him.

Finally, release came on a whoosh of a cry. She collapsed on top of him, breathing hard. She closed her eyes, felt his long strong arms cuddle around her. Felt his kiss on her brow.

That was the last thing she knew…until the rock-and-roll ring of his cell phone startled them both.

Amanda didn't know what time it was. Only that Mike popped awake as if shot with a bullet. Still, he took the time to ease her on her side before jerking across the bed, patting the floor until he located his pants, found and flipped on the phone.

She knew it was about Teddy. What else? Her blurry eyes eventually made it to the bedside clock. 3:00 a.m.

Definitely Teddy.

The conversation was hard to transcribe. Someone on the other end was talking; Mike's voice sounded as if he were talking through mud. "Okay. Okay. Okay. I'll be right there."

When he snapped off the cell, she said, "Ill? Or scared?"

"Ill. Just woke up. Rash and a fever." He was already out of bed, pulling on jeans. "At least he didn't wake up from being afraid. He was making it the whole night. My mom's best guess is chicken pox. I could have sworn he had every vaccine known to the universe. I thought kids couldn't get any of those 'spot' diseases anymore."

He'd immediately gone into dad mode, which she completely understood. When a child was sick, parental instincts took precedence over everything else. She didn't expect him to be thinking of her... yet the minute he pulled on his shirt, he leaned over and kissed the side of her neck. Slowly. Tenderly. Softly.

Before swearing, and grumbling that he had to go.

"But we have unfinished business, Red. And don't you forget it."

She smiled in the darkness, closed her eyes.

She thought she'd sleep...not only had Mike completely worn her out, but the day had been long and traumatic before that. Yet moments later, her eyes popped wide-open.

The day *had* been traumatic, the custody hearing agonizing. She'd been building character and strength and some skills, she'd thought. All blown away when she couldn't get the judge to listen about Molly. She'd left the stupid hearing feeling beyond inadequate.

Now, though, it occurred to her that was kind of how she'd felt after Mike bailed her out of her plumbing mess. She'd been so clueless. Because she'd *been* clueless. He'd been a hero for her that day.

The blackest night slowly brightened, turned into a pre-dawn dusty charcoal…then finally the pearl fog of a new day. It was still only five o'clock. She faced the window, from the pillow where Mike had laid his head, curled up tight. Now she got it. He hadn't stopped over by accident with that god-awful whisky.

He'd been her hero.

Again.

He hadn't changed the outcome of the stupid hearing. But he'd made her put it in a different perspective. He'd known perfectly well what he was doing. He'd planned it.

By five-thirty, she was biting her nails…and she hadn't bitten her nails since she was six. This was precisely how they'd screwed up before. That's what happened when you had kids, of course. Instead of being able to cuddle and talk things out and just *be* together after making love…they'd had to separate. And in the hours apart, they'd both frozen up.

Both of them. Not just her. He'd frozen up, too.

She felt as if she were on the cusp of grasping it

all—grasping what really mattered, about her, about him, about the two of them…when suddenly she heard Molly cry out.

There was no way Teddy was staying at his parents' house. None. Teddy was beside himself crying when Mike showed up…and burning up, as well.

His mom never freaked in a crisis, but she was clearly upset. "I know what to do for a sick child, Mike, for heaven's sake. It has all the symptoms of chicken pox. Nothing worse. But I just couldn't seem to comfort him. All he wanted was you."

"It's okay. I'll get him home." Teddy immediately simmered down—at least temporarily—once Mike picked him up.

Except, Mike was the one shaken up after that. Teddy's little body was so darned hot. Mike wrapped him in the sheet he'd been sleeping in, added a blanket, strapped the whole bundle into the truck and took off for home.

Before daylight, he'd called the new pediatrician, the old pediatrician, the E.R. They all gave him the same answer. The pinpoint-size spray of spots on Teddy's chest and tummy were symptomatic of chicken pox. So was the 102-degree fever. And a mild case of chicken pox was running through the county. They gave him the rundown on the course of the disease, things he could try, what to expect for the next ten days.

They all said the same thing.

This was a normal childhood illness, nothing to worry about.

Right. His kid was miserable, threw up the child's fever reducer, didn't want to sleep, just wanted to be held on his dad's lap in the recliner. Eventually Cat joined them. Then Slugger.

He wanted to call Amanda. Couldn't—without dislodging his entire family. And then she called, sometime early in the morning. He couldn't reach the phone fast enough, and the answering machine picked up.

"Mike...Molly came down with chicken pox. I'm guessing if you're dealing with a rash and fever, your Teddy has the same thing. Call if you need a hand." Then her softer voice. "We'll catch up. You can count on it."

He brooded on that. For him, their night together had been an Armageddon...but there was every reason to fear she wouldn't take it in a positive way. Hell. It could look to her like he'd plied her with liquor and been insensitive to the custody hearing thing she'd been through.

He made red Jell-O soup and scrambled eggs, then blue Jell-O soup, then finally got the hang of making the Jell-O gel. But then it gelled so tight that you could turn the bowl upside down and it wouldn't come out. Teddy asked for peanut butter and jelly—which he promptly threw up. Mike microwaved chicken noodle soup. Then more scrambled eggs. Then he ran out of Jell-O and scrambled eggs.

The tiny dots formed blisters two days later. Teddy's fever broke, but now he was itching and miserable and crabby.

Mike played trucks. And watched cartoons. And read books. And played fish. He coated the kid with everything he had in the medicine cabinet to stop the itching.

When he heard the knock on the door, he wasn't sure if it was Tuesday or Thursday, what month, what year. It was daylight. That's all he was sure of.

He opened the door, squinted at the sudden sharp sunlight…saw Amanda. Well, mostly what he saw was her flaming hair and shocked expression.

"Holy kamoly. You look *horrible*. Why didn't you call me? I was—"

He wasn't coherent. Wasn't going to be coherent again. Maybe ever. So he just blurted out what he needed to say. "I wasn't trying to get you drunk."

"I never thought you were."

"I didn't mean to be so…physical."

"Of course you did. That's you. You'll always be more fantastic with action, especially that action— than talk. Chitchat isn't your thing. No sweat." She closed the door and took a long gander at his living area. "You are such a dimwit. Why didn't you tell me you were in trouble?" Then she took an even longer gander at him. "You haven't shaved. You look as if you haven't slept. You look as if—"

"It's been horrible," he confirmed.

"Molly's taking a nap. My mom came over to watch her for a couple hours. I needed to get out to the grocery store, and I came over to see if I could pick up anything for you two." She raised her eyebrows. "No point in asking, I can see. It's obvious you need everything. Let's see how good you are at following orders."

"What orders?"

By nightfall, Mike figured she was akin to a cyclone. They were at her house by then. The kids were in pajamas in front of the TV. Both had had oatmeal baths, rubdowns, a liberal application of calamine, then dressed in their pj's. They'd gobbled down toasted cheese sandwiches, then lemonade, then small bowls of sorbet.

Nobody was crying. Nobody was whining. Both kids looked a pinch away from going to sleep for the night.

"I think," Amanda said quietly, as she handed him a serious bowl of chili sprinkled with sour cream and melted cheddar, "that you and Teddy should take the spare room tonight. Molly can sleep in with me. My guess is that you really need a night's sleep, and I can handle a round if the kids need someone in the night."

She could handle both kids behind her back. And him. They'd stayed at his place until she'd transformed it. The dirty dishes went away. The Jell-O bowls disappeared. The heap of messy cutlery seemed to all fit in the washer. She'd stayed with Teddy while he showered and found clean clothes. Then she'd herded them to her place—kicked her mom out—and started in with the little ones. The baths, the cooking and feeding. The calm, no-nonsense orders. Even Slugger and Darling obeyed her. They were sacked out by their respective charges by the couch.

"I think that's too much trouble for you," he said.

"What's the trouble? Both of us will end up losing sleep if we stay in separate houses. This way we can run relay for each other. Each get a solid stretch of sleep."

She sounded totally reasonable, but Mike wanted time with her. *Real* time. Not time like this. He couldn't guess what she was thinking or feeling—about him. About them.

But he caved about the sleepover, and when he settled Teddy in the upstairs room around eight o'clock that evening, Teddy begged him to sack out next to him. He did, for just a few minutes.

The next time he surfaced, Teddy was still sleeping soundly, and the wall clock claimed it was 6:00 a.m.

He'd slept ten solid hours.

And there was only one thing he wanted or needed—and that was to find Amanda.

Chapter Thirteen

Mike was quiet, descending the stairs, unsure if Amanda or Molly were sleeping—not wanting to wake either of them if they were still asleep. But when he glanced outside...there was a slim, white, unforgettable leg stretched out on a lawn chair.

The morning was cool, with a wispy mist dancing over the grass, hiding in and out of bushes. The sun had a beat of warmth, more promise than reality this early. She'd put a bowl of strawberries on the glass table, a carafe of coffee with a spare mug that he strongly suspected was for him. Both his dog and hers were snoozing at her feet.

She was wearing easy clothes, that kind of green

she liked, in a loose, soft top paired with jeans. Her feet were bare. So was her face.

When he opened the door, she immediately looked up and smiled. Then motioned to the mug.

"I figured coffee might be the first thing you wanted."

"That's it," he said firmly. "I love you forever. Don't fight it. You're going to have to marry me."

"You know what? I was thinking the same thing."

He almost sputtered on the first sip—when he was downright desperate for that caffeine. She clearly liked it that she so easily rattled him. She watched him sit in the chair next to hers, put a foot up before speaking.

"When I woke up three mornings ago," she said quietly, "I thought…maybe you were into payback. That you were doing the same thing to me…that you believed I'd done to you."

"Run that by me again. A little slower. A *lot* slower, Amanda."

So she went slower. "The first time we made love… you thought I was doing a hit-and-run. That I was willing to sleep with you. But still keep a distance."

He wasn't sure what the balance was between quicksand versus honesty. So he just motioned her to go on.

"So when I woke up three mornings ago…I started worrying…at first…that you were doing just that.

Startling me with a seduction. You didn't ask first. You just took charge."

"Amanda—" He got it. Quicksand or not, he had to get the whole truth out there, no matter what it cost him. Too much was at stake to risk less.

"Hear me out. I figured it out, Mike. Your coming on to me took a ton of courage…just like the night I came on to you was the biggest risk I'd ever taken. I've been trying to be a different woman than I was before. So that first night, it wasn't about sex. Or just about sex. It was about my being strong enough and honest enough to admit I wanted you. And to ask for what I wanted and needed, loud and strong."

His turn then. "Three nights ago, I knew something bad had happened at the hearing. I could see it in your face, your eyes. I didn't how to help. I just knew…I wanted you to turn to me when something bad or sad happened. No matter when or how or what it was. I *hated* it. That you felt so bad."

She put down her coffee, leaned forward. She lifted her hands toward him and he took them. Their knees touched. Their palms nested together. She said carefully, "Mike. I don't want to be a leaner. Or a needer."

"I know that bugs you. But I don't see it. I never saw it. You're smart. You're a general and a diplomat in a crisis. You're the best mom on the planet. When a situation's tough, you don't run, you dive in—wherever, whenever. Do whatever it takes."

She frowned, as if it never occurred to her that someone would see her that way. "I was just raised... so helpless."

"That may be true, Red. But that's not character. It's just circumstance. A person doesn't start out the first day of medical school doing brain surgery. It takes some time and practice."

"You respected that before I did."

He hesitated, long and hard. Reached for more coffee. Still hesitated. Her eyes were on his face, her expression patient, waiting. Apparently she wanted him to lay out something tough. Offhand, he couldn't think of any way to avoid it—particularly if he wanted to win her. And he wanted that more than life.

"Okay...from my side of the fence now...I let something loose the other night."

"I know. You shared some of your precious Talisker."

"That's true. But not that. I was worried about... Well, I don't know how to say this. I just don't seem to do certain things...in a fastidious way."

"Fastidious?"

Okay. So he didn't know the right word. The delicate, ladylike word. "You know," he said edgily. "There's a place for *please* and *thank you*. Maybe even a place for that language in bed. But I can't promise any aptitude for...finesse."

"This is about your ex, isn't it." She didn't frame a

question, because there wasn't one. She already knew that answer.

"Yeah. When she picked up with George... I don't know how to say it. But she made me feel like I was a bull. Insensitive. Not the tidy kind under the covers. It's my reality. I like the smells, the sweat, the sounds."

"Mike?"

"What?"

"I'm sorry your ex is such a prissy woman, handsome. But personally, I think it's obvious that you're always going to be dark French roast, not decaf."

"Well...maybe I need to know if you're into that dark French roast thing."

"Hmm." She appeared to consider. "After the two intensive samples I've had...I have to say I can't ever imagine wanting decaf, ever. Why settle for bland when you can have it all?"

"That's it," he said, and pulled her from her chair onto his lap. He couldn't wait any longer to touch her. Hold her. "I told you I loved you, Amanda. And I meant it from the heart and soul both."

She lifted her face, anticipating his kiss. That first connection was so sweet, so needed, so cherished that he felt his heart opening, wide enough to let the sun in.

His sun was her.

Naturally, seconds later, the dogs got up and barked. Then Molly stormed outside, followed by

Teddy. Both their kids were still polka-dotted. Neither seemed to find it strange that their parents were snuggled together. They just both climbed on. Then came the dogs. Darling fit on top, but Slugger couldn't jump that high, and started baying his unhappiness.

Amanda started laughing...then so did he.

"How on earth are we going to keep all this straight?" he demanded.

"That's easy," she murmured. "Everything is yours, mine and ours."

And kissed him again.

The August afternoon was crazy-hot...hot enough that Mike felt justified hiding in the basement. That was, until Amanda found him.

"Out," she said simply.

"I don't think I can do it."

"Out," she repeated. He gave in—Amanda knew he would eventually. "I can't believe a big strong guy like you would be afraid of a few kids."

"I never heard of a meet-and-greet for four-year-olds. And as far as I can tell, the whole thing's terrifying."

It wasn't. It was a super way for the kids to meet some other children their age before preschool actually started. Both yards were decorated with balloons and tables, both places had snacks and drinks. Precisely between the houses, there was a hired balloon maker...making animal balloons for each child. In

Mike's yard, groups congregated who wanted to do the worm-and-frog thing. In Amanda's, there was a twirling contest, requiring a lot of girls wearing tutus and crowns.

Amanda had hoped a good handful would come to the impromptu gig. Instead…she counted over thirty kids, not counting moms and neighbors. "Talk about a success," she murmured.

"All your doing. I still can't believe we're both surviving suburbia."

She lifted her head, saw his expression. "You've come to love it, haven't you?"

"Love it—yeah. In spite of myself. But we have an awful lot to sort out, Amanda. Which house do you want to live in? Are both of us going to work? How are we going to manage all the grandparents? The ex's?"

"Yes," she said, as if that were an answer.

"Yes?"

"Uh-huh. There was a time I wanted perfect, Mike. Now I realize what I was looking for back then was shallow and boring. Never again. I want complications. I want messes. I want challenges. Are we going to have fun creating our lives together, or what?"

"You said it. Bring it on, Red." He grinned, bent down to kiss her nose…and naturally, was interrupted by the sound of a scream. Molly's.

In her most dramatic voice, Molly announced to

the world in general, "Guess *what!* Princess just had a kitten. On my bed!"

"Uh-oh," Mike murmured.

Amanda laughed again. "Just one more thing that's going to be yours, mine and ours. What could possibly be better than that?"

"Nothing in this world," he agreed, and swung his arm around her shoulder.

* * * * *

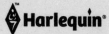
Harlequin®

REQUEST YOUR FREE BOOKS!

2 FREE NOVELS PLUS 2 FREE GIFTS!

♦ Harlequin®

SPECIAL EDITION

Life, Love & Family

YES! Please send me 2 FREE Harlequin Special Edition® novels and my 2 FREE gifts (gifts are worth about $10). After receiving them, if I don't wish to receive any more books, I can return the shipping statement marked "cancel." If I don't cancel, I will receive 6 brand-new novels every month and be billed just $4.24 per book in the U.S. or $4.99 per book in Canada. That's a saving of at least 15% off the cover price! It's quite a bargain! Shipping and handling is just 50¢ per book in the U.S. and 75¢ per book in Canada.* I understand that accepting the 2 free books and gifts places me under no obligation to buy anything. I can always return a shipment and cancel at any time. Even if I never buy another book, the two free books and gifts are mine to keep forever.

235/335 SDN FC7H

Name	(PLEASE PRINT)

Address	Apt. #

City	State/Prov.	Zip/Postal Code

Signature (if under 18, a parent or guardian must sign)

Mail to the Reader Service:
IN U.S.A.: P.O. Box 1867, Buffalo, NY 14240-1867
IN CANADA: P.O. Box 609, Fort Erie, Ontario L2A 5X3

Not valid for current subscribers to Harlequin Special Edition books.

Want to try two free books from another line?
Call 1-800-873-8635 or visit www.ReaderService.com.

* Terms and prices subject to change without notice. Prices do not include applicable taxes. Sales tax applicable in N.Y. Canadian residents will be charged applicable taxes. Offer not valid in Quebec. This offer is limited to one order per household. All orders subject to credit approval. Credit or debit balances in a customer's account(s) may be offset by any other outstanding balance owed by or to the customer. Please allow 4 to 6 weeks for delivery. Offer available while quantities last.

Your Privacy—The Reader Service is committed to protecting your privacy. Our Privacy Policy is available online at www.ReaderService.com or upon request from the Reader Service.

We make a portion of our mailing list available to reputable third parties that offer products we believe may interest you. If you prefer that we not exchange your name with third parties, or if you wish to clarify or modify your communication preferences, please visit us at www.ReaderService.com/consumerschoice or write to us at Reader Service Preference Service, P.O. Box 9062, Buffalo, NY 14269. Include your complete name and address.

*With an evil force hell-bent on destruction,
two enemies must unite to find a truth that turns
all-too-personal when passions collide.*

*Enjoy a sneak peek in Jenna Kernan's next installment
in her original* TRACKER *series, GHOST STALKER,
available in May, only from Harlequin Nocturne.*

"**W**ho are you?" he snarled.

Jessie lifted her chin. "Your better."

His smile was cold. "Such arrogance could only come from a Niyanoka."

She nodded. "Why are you here?"

"I don't know." He glanced about her room. "I asked the birds to take me to a healer."

"And they have done so. Is that *all* you asked?"

"No. To lead them away from my friends." His eyes fluttered and she saw them roll over white.

Jessie straightened, preparing to flee, but he roused himself and mastered the momentary weakness. His eyes snapped open, locking on her.

Her heart hammered as she inched back.

"Lead who away?" she whispered, suddenly afraid of the answer.

"The ghosts. Nagi sent them to attack me so I would bring them to her."

The wolf must be deranged because Nagi did not send ghosts to attack living creatures. He captured the evil ones after their death if they refused to walk the Way of Souls, forcing them to face judgment.

"Her? The healer you seek is also female?"

"Michaela. She's Niyanoka, like you. The last Seer of Souls and Nagi wants her dead."

Jessie fell back to her seat on the carpet as the possibility of this ricocheted in her brain. Could it be true?

"Why should I believe you?" But she knew why. His black aura, the part that said he had been touched by death. Only a ghost could do that. But it made no sense.

Why would Nagi hunt one of her people and why would a Skinwalker want to protect her? She had been trained from birth to hate the Skinwalkers, to consider them a threat.

His intent blue eyes pinned her. Jessie felt her mouth go dry as she considered the impossible. Could the trickster be speaking the truth? Great Mystery, what evil was this?

She stared in astonishment. There was only one way to find her answers. But she had never even met a Skinwalker before and so did not even know if they dreamed.

But if he dreamed, she would have her chance to learn the truth.

*Look for GHOST STALKER by Jenna Kernan,
available May only from Harlequin Nocturne,
wherever books and ebooks are sold.*

HNEXP0511